Statistics

How to Handle and

Statistics for Social Sciences

How to Handle and Analyse Data in Social Sciences

Ian Hosker
BEd(Hons) MSc MInstLM FRSA

www.**studymates**.co.uk

Typeset by PDQ Typesetting, Newcastle-under-Lyme, Staffordshire.
Printed and bound in Europe.

Contents

List of illustrations

Preface

This book has been written for social scientists with limited or no knowledge of statistics. The aim is not to make you an expert statistician, but to provide you with a statistical toolkit so that you can undertake any quantitative survey work. Many students of the social sciences are more concerned with understanding social and psychological events, but in order to do this may need to undertake quantitative research work.

In that context, statistics is needed to support your hypotheses, and so it is more important to know what techniques you need to use, their significance and limitations of use. Statistics is the servant of social researchers, not their ruler.

This book:

▶ explains the principles of statistical techniques, not their mathematical derivations
▶ explains the techniques and when to use them
▶ avoids complex mathematical formulae (technology makes their use unnecessary unless you are a theoretical statistician)
▶ assumes you will have access to computer software that will carry out the tedious tasks associated with calculations.

In other words, the emphasis is on learning appropriate techniques to adopt for any given purpose. This allows your skill to be reserved for the choice of technique and the interpretation of results, and not wasted on routine number-crunching.

Structure of the book

The book is organised so that it takes you through the process of data analysis. It covers:

▶ the theory of probability that underpins data analysis
▶ using probability theory to create a representative sample for your survey

► managing your data once you have collected it
► identifying a research question and converting that into measurable variables
► developing scales and indices as comparative measures for variables that are not directly quantifiable
► designing your questionnaire to ensure reliability, validity, and to motivate respondents
► summarising your data after collection to examine its main characteristics
► developing and testing hypotheses
► using statistical techniques to explore relationships between variables, and to test their statistical significance.

Target courses

This text has not been narrowly written for one particular syllabus or course. Many courses from A level, to undergraduate and even postgraduate level in the social sciences – require some knowledge of statistics. That knowledge frequently does not involve complex derivations. Examples of courses where this text will be of value are:

Access courses	Social science
	Psychology
A level	Sociology
	Psychology
Degree	Sociology/Applied Social Sciences
	Psychology
Postgraduate	Applied Social Sciences
	Research Methods

There are extra pdf files that are available via the internet for free. To claim your files please send your name and address to info@study mates.co.uk

Ian Hosker
ianhosker@studymates.co.uk

1

Probability – The Underlying Principles

One-minute Overview – Probability is used to make a judgement about the likelihood of a particular event. To do this we first need to work out what all the possible outcomes might be. The probability of your particular outcome occurring is the proportion of the total possibilities it represents. Probability underpins everything a statistician does; it is used to assess the reliability of judgements based on statistical analysis. In this chapter you will learn about:

▶ probably or probability?
▶ the likelihood of an event
▶ the probability of multiple events
▶ the addition and multiplication rules
▶ the probability of failure
▶ sources of error

Probably or probability?

Probably

In an everyday, non-mathematical context, we always make judgements about the likelihood of a particular event. Where a number of possible outcomes exist, we assess which is the most likely under any given set of circumstances. For example, when I travel to work each Monday morning, I notice that the traffic is usually heavier, and the journey correspondingly slower, at the time I normally travel than it is at the same time Tuesday to Friday! If there has been a heavy snowfall overnight the traffic is even heavier and slower moving.

The judgement that is being made here is based on my experience of driving to work along a route that I have used for almost 8 years. I believe that on balance this behaviour is more likely to happen than not to happen, because it has been the case *in the past*. I am using historical evidence to predict a future event, and assume this event will *probably* happen.

Probably is an intuitive assessment that all sentient animals make in relation to everyday existence. It is part of our survival kit. The process becomes fine-tuned by exposure to the events over time.

Probability – the mathematics of uncertainty

There is a problem in making judgements about the likelihood of whether an event will or will not happen:

▶ *Problem* – Each individual will arrive at a different assessment of the situation because of the way he or she interprets the observations.

Because of this, errors – or bias – are always built in to observations and interpretations of events. You cannot be absolutely sure of what you have observed; you will be even less sure of being able to predict a future event on the basis of uncertain observations of past events.

Karl Friedrich Gauss, at the end of the eighteenth century, worked out that all human observations are subject to numerous sources of error. His work has formed the basis of statistics theory ever since.

In the next chapter, we will look at the nature of a **population** in more detail. It is sufficient to say here that:

▶ *The probability* of an event occurring, or of an observation being accurate, is the mathematical expression of the certainty of accuracy.

So, I might be 95% certain that I will be late arriving at work next time the dual events of a Monday morning and a snowfall coincide! But, there is still a 5% chance that I won't be late!

The likelihood of an event

Calculating the probability of an event

The implication is that there must be a mathematical route to arriving at such a conclusion. There is. We will explore the route, and the underlying assumptions, in the rest of this chapter. It is important to grasp the underlying argument in order to understand where it all comes from. In fact, you will need this understanding throughout the book.

The simplest way of explaining probability is to use the example of tossing a coin: will it result in a heads or a tails? Things become more complicated when you throw a die, because there are not two but six possible outcomes.

Spinning a coin

All things being equal (see **Sources of error**), the coin is just as likely to land on heads as it is on tails. There are two possible outcomes; each alternative is as likely as the other. The *probability* of it being heads is therefore said to be 0.5, with the same probability for tails. Probability may be expressed:

1. as a decimal, for example 0.5
2. as percentage, for example a 50% chance.

The total probability of all the possible outcomes adds up to 1, in other words 100%. Things are never that simple, of course. If the coin lands on heads after the first spin, it does not necessarily land on tails after the second spin.

▶ *Key point* – This is because each spin is a separate event. The probability of landing on heads is still 0.5 so it is just as likely to land on heads again.

Table 1.1 shows the actual outcomes of 500 spins of a coin. The table shows the results of each spin in consecutive order in the columns (labelled 1st 50, etc). This is mentioned here because we will shortly look at the relationship between successive results. The table also shows the total number of heads and tails recorded and also expresses these as a percentage of the total.

If the probability of each of the two possible outcomes of spinning a coin is 0.5, or 50%, then you might expect the table to be made up of 50% heads and 50% tails. In fact – and this is not a fix – a coin was spun 500 times to produce this table, the actual result is very close to that expectation. 50.4% of outcomes were heads, and 49.6% of outcomes were tails.

The basic method of calculating a probability

The basic method of calculating the probability of an event's outcome is deceptively simple. The deception lies in the assumptions we make,

Table 1.1 Results of 500 Spins of a Coin

1st 50	2nd 50	3rd 50	4th 50	5th 50	6th 50	7th 50	8th 50	9th 50	10th 50
H	T	T	H	T	H	H	H	T	H
T	T	T	T	H	H	T	T	T	T
H	H	H	H	T	H	T	T	H	T
H	T	T	T	H	T	H	H	H	H
H	T	H	H	T	T	T	H	H	H
T	H	T	T	H	H	H	H	T	T
T	T	H	H	H	T	T	T	T	T
T	T	T	T	H	T	H	H	H	T
T	H	H	H	T	H	T	T	T	T
T	H	T	H	H	T	T	H	T	T
T	H	T	T	H	H	H	T	T	H
T	T	T	H	H	T	H	T	H	T
T	H	H	T	T	T	T	H	T	T
T	H	H	T	H	H	T	T	T	T
T	H	H	H	T	H	T	H	H	T
H	H	T	T	T	T	T	H	T	T
H	H	H	T	T	T	T	T	H	T
H	H	H	T	H	T	T	H	H	H
H	H	T	H	H	T	H	T	T	H
H	H	T	H	H	H	H	H	T	T
T	T	T	H	H	H	T	H	H	H
T	H	H	T	H	H	T	H	H	T
H	H	H	H	T	H	T	H	H	T
T	H	T	H	H	T	H	H	H	H
T	T	H	H	T	T	H	H	T	T
T	H	T	H	H	T	T	H	T	T
H	H	H	T	T	H	H	H	H	H
T	H	H	H	H	T	T	H	H	T
T	H	H	H	T	T	T	T	H	T
H	T	T	H	H	T	H	H	T	H
T	T	T	T	H	H	T	H	H	T
T	H	T	H	T	T	T	T	T	T
T	H	T	T	T	T	H	T	H	T
T	T	T	T	H	T	H	T	H	H
T	T	T	T	H	T	H	T	H	H
T	H	T	H	H	H	T	H	T	H
H	T	H	H	H	H	T	H	H	H
H	H	H	H	H	H	H	H	T	H
H	T	T	T	T	T	H	T	H	H
H	T	T	H	H	H	T	H	T	H
H	T	T	T	H	T	H	T	H	H
H	H	H	H	T	T	H	H	H	T
T	H	H	T	H	T	T	H	H	T
H	T	T	T	H	H	T	T	H	T
H	H	T	H	T	T	T	T	H	T
H	T	H	T	T	H	H	H	T	T
H	T	H	H	T	H	H	T	H	T
H	T	H	T	H	H	T	T	T	H

Number of Heads	253	% Heads		50.6%	
Number of Tails	247	% Tails		49.4%	

but we will come to this later. To calculate the probability of any particular outcome, you need to first determine the number of possible outcomes. The probability is then a fraction of 100%.

In the case of a coin, there are only two possible outcomes heads or tails so the probability of each of these outcomes is 0.5 (50%) as was described above. But what about the probability of getting a six when a die is thrown?

A die has six faces, and so six possible outcomes. Therefore, the probability of throwing a six is:

    0.166 recurring   (0.17 if we round up)   or 16.67%

▶ *Key point* – Probability is a straightforward proportion calculation.

Predicting the future?

You know the probability of either a heads or a tails, but what you will *never* know is the outcome before actually spinning the coin. You can also assess risk of failure (i.e. 50% chance of not getting a heads next time). On that basis of knowledge you can make a decision about a bet. If the last spin was a tails, there is no guarantee that the next will be a tails. The two spins are completely independent of each other.

You can see this in table 1.1. In the first column, spins 6 to 16 produced a remarkable run on tails. This could not have been predicted. Indeed, as I was spinning the coin, I was concerned about what was happening and wondered if the coin was 'loaded'!

▶ *Key point* – Probability cannot provide a definitive mechanism for predicting an outcome. Probability does help you assess the likelihood of an outcome, and so informs your decision-making process. If the *probability* of an outcome is high, then you may think it is *probably* worth taking a risk with a particular decision.

Later in this book we will look at **statistical significance**. We will use probability theory to assess whether or not an outcome is really the result of some factor or other under investigation, or is more likely to have happened by chance or random act.

The probability of multiple events

If you have two coins or two dice you will increase the number of possible outcomes. If you have only one coin or die, you may still want to know the probability of different combinations of outcomes (e.g. a heads following on consecutively from a tails, or of achieving 3 head out of 10 spins). The way you calculate the probability of an outcome depends on the relationship between the different events.

For the sake of visual simplicity, probability is usually represented by P or p. This shorthand convention will be followed throughout this book. To distinguish between the probability of one event and another, the event itself will be represented by $_{(event)}$. For example, the probability of a coin landing on heads might be represented by:

$$P_{(H)}$$

Consider the following examples that illustrate the basic rules of calculating the probability of any event.

The addition rule

When possible outcomes are mutually exclusive

You throw a die and want it to land on 6. It cannot land on any of the other numbers as well. This makes each possible outcome *mutually exclusive* i.e. they cannot happen at the same time.

Since there are six possible outcomes, the probability is 0.17 (i.e. 1/6). But what is the probability of throwing either a 1 or a 6? On a single throw it is not possible to have both 1 and 6 as an outcome (it has to be one or the other). These outcomes are therefore *mutually exclusive*. Each has an equal chance of occurring. The probability is calculated by adding the individual probabilities, like this:

$$P_{(1 \text{ or } 6)} = P_{(1)} + P_{(6)} = 1/6 + 1/6 = 1/3 = 0.33 = 33.3\%$$

Gaining a 1 or a 6 represents two of the six possible outcomes – a 1 in 3 chance. The corresponding probability of not throwing a 1 or a 6 will be the probability of failure, i.e. 0.67 or a 2 in 3 chance.

▶ *Key point* – Where the outcomes are each mutually exclusive, the probability of gaining any one of two or more possible outcomes is calculated by adding the probability of each option.

Where possible outcomes are not mutually exclusive

Now look at a slightly different example where the range of possible outcomes is more complex. The example used to illustrate this set of circumstances is a deck of playing cards. Figure 1.1 shows the scenario in diagrammatic form. If you have difficulty following the logic of what is about to be described, look at the illustration for clarification.

▶ *The problem* – What is the probability of drawing either a spade or a king when picking a card from the pack?

Begin by assuming that the pack has been thoroughly shuffled and that the position of any card is not known, and that the selection of the card from the pack will be a random act. We know that, of the 52 cards in the pack, 13 are spades and 4 are kings. On the face of it, you might assume it safe to calculate the probability of drawing either a king or a spade as:

$$P_{(\text{Spade or King})} = P_{(\text{Spade})} + P_{(\text{King})} = 13/52 + 4/52 = 17/52 = 0.33$$

...and you would be *wrong!*

Looking at figure 1.1, it is not hard to see why. While 17 cards in the pack will be spades or kings, one of these is both. In other words, *the selection of a spade or a king is not a mutually exclusive event*. It is possible to draw a card that is both a spade and a king. The condition of *either* a spade *or* a king would not be met if the king of spades were selected.

The correct calculation for this event is:

$$P_{(S \text{ or } K)} = P_{(S)} + P_{(\overline{K})} P_{(S \& K)} = 13/52 + 4/52 \overline{} 1/52 = 16/52 = 0.31$$

This may seem an insignificant difference, but at other times the difference might be larger. This provides a generalised equation for events were the possible outcomes might or might not be mutually exclusive. This is:

$$P_{(a \text{ or } b)} = P_{(a)} + P_{(\overline{b})} P_{(a \text{ and } b)}$$

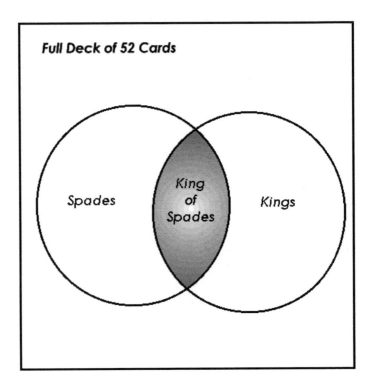

Figure 1.1. A Venn diagram.

Of course, if a and b are mutually exclusive, $P_{(a\ and\ b)}$ is zero and so doesn't count.

The type of diagram shown in figure 1.1 is called a **Venn diagram.** It is often a good idea to draw a Venn diagram when you have a problem of this type, because it will help you sort out the possible outcomes and determine mutually and non-mutually exclusive events.

The multiplication rule

Two events may be dependent upon each other – that is to say, the outcome of a subsequent event depends on the outcome of the previous one. In this case the probability of those events occurring is calculated rather differently. Here is a simple example.

If two coins are spun, the possible outcomes are as follows:

Outcome		Probability
H	T	1 in 4 (0.25)
T	H	1 in 4 (0.25)
H	H	1 in 4 (0.25)
T	T	1 in 4 (0.25)

What is the probability of getting a heads followed by a tails? Clearly, if the first spin leads to a tails, the scenario has failed. It has also failed if, after a successful first spin, the second spin results in a heads. The difference between this situation and those described above, is that the heads followed by the tails counts as one event – one outcome – not two, but success is dependent on the correct sequence.

Look again at the list above. You can see there are four possible outcomes, or combinations of heads and tails. Therefore, the probability is 0.25 (1 in 4). In these circumstances of mutual dependence you determine the probability of the outcome by multiplying the probabilities of each individual part of the event:

1. The probability of spinning a heads on the first go is 0.5.

2. If the coin is spun again, the probability of spinning a tails is also 0.5 (since the outcome of the second spin is not affected by the first).

You calculate the probability of a sequence of heads followed by tails like this:

$$P_{(H \text{ followed by } T)} = P_{(H)} \times P_{(T)} = 0.5 \times 0.5 = 0.25 = 25\%$$

Consider a variation of this. Suppose you are playing around with a pack of cards. To pass the time you want to know the probability of drawing three cards in the following sequence: red, black, red. After drawing each card you put it to one side away from the pack so that it cannot be drawn again. There will now be fewer cards as you continue to draw from the pack. There are 26 red and 26 black cards to begin with. The probability of drawing a red card first is:

$$P_{(R)} = 26/52 = 0.5$$

There are now 25 red and 26 black cards (51 cards altogether). So, the probability of drawing a black card next is:

$$P_{(B)} = 26/51 = 0.51$$

Finally, there are 25 red and 25 black (50 cards), so the probability of drawing a red next is again:

$$P_{(R2)} = 25/50 = 0.5$$

Notice, in the second draw, there is a slightly higher probability of drawing a black card because there is one more than red. The probability of gaining this sequence is calculated thus:

$$P_{(RBR)} = P_{(R)} + P_{(B)} + P_{(R2)} = 0.5 \text{ x } 0.51 \text{ x } 0.5 = 0.13$$

The probability of failure

If we can calculate the probability of an event happening, then we can also work out the probability of it not happening. So, the probability of throwing a die and it landing on six is:

$$P_{(6)} = 1/6 = 0.17$$

Then the probability of it not landing on 6 must be:

$$P_{(not\ 6)} = 5/6 = 0.83$$

Why? – because the sum of the probability of all outcomes must equal 1 (i.e. 100%). This is represented by a general equation:

$$P_{(failure)} = 1 - P_{(success)}$$

$$P_{(not\ 6)} = 1 - 1/6 = 5/6 = 0.83$$

Unfortunately, unless the probability of success is rather high, it is often more tempting to bet on failure, a somewhat depressing and negative position. However, this fact is important in quantitative analysis in the social sciences (or any subject requiring statistical techniques), because it is necessary to show that the probability of any event or relationship being studied is very high indeed. This is needed to give us a high degree of confidence in the accuracy of the findings.

This point will be considered in more detail later in the book when the concept of **statistical significance** is explained.

Sources of error

The assumption of 'no bias'

It is important to realise that there is an underlying assumption of 'no bias'. In other words, the likelihood of an outcome is only related to the number of possible outcomes and there are no other factors acting to influence the result. In other words it is a **random event**.

▶ *Example* – The weight of a coin may not be evenly distributed throughout because of its shape, and this may influence the way it lands when tossed. If that were the case, then you would expect to find a distorted proportion of heads and tails. Equally, if a die were 'loaded' so that the weight was concentrated towards one side, you would expect to find a disproportionate amount of outcomes where the die landed to reveal the face opposite the excess weight.

However, in statistics, as in life, nothing is ever that simple. Because each throw of the die or spin of the coin is an independent act, the outcome of any one throw or spin is not affected by the outcome of the previous one. And here is the rub! Just because you throw a six on ten consecutive throws of the die, it does not necessarily mean that the die is loaded. Every outcome is possible. In statistics you are concerned with the likelihood of such an outcome. The probability of this happening is extremely low (0.000000017), but it is still a possible outcome.

In this situation, you are faced with a problem. Do you really believe that this could have happened if the die were 'honest'? Of course, it could, but the balance of probability is very much against it happening. However, because it is a possible outcome, there is uncertainty. This **uncertainty factor** is used to make judgements about possible interpretations of statistical data.

Measurement errors

Other possible errors that can distort results are simple measurement mistakes. Straightforward lack of accuracy in measuring or calculating or coding a response in a questionnaire will introduce unfortunate errors into the work.

▶ *Random errors* – are those that result from a single mistake, or a small number of unrelated errors. For example, a decimal point might be in the wrong place, or an extra zero has been included, or a questionnaire response might have been miscoded because of a momentary lapse of concentration. These can often be spotted and corrected, especially if they are way out. If the data is plotted on a graph, a pattern may emerge, but one or two points on the graph may lie well off the line or curve. This may be because it is a mistake and is called a **rogue value.**

▶ *Systematic errors* – are often rather more difficult to spot because they are the result of an error that becomes repeated throughout a whole set of data. For example, a particular response in a questionnaire may be coded throughout as 1 by one person, while someone else may put a different interpretation on the response and always code it 2.

We will come back to this subject again, but do be aware that errors are a real and ever present likelihood. All statistical work does require very careful scrutiny before putting any trust in it!

▶ *An absolute rule* – Always question the reliability and validity of statistical data. (Reliability and validity are two terms that will be explained in chapter 2).

Tutorial: helping you learn

Progress questions

1. A coin is spun 10 times and results in 9 heads and 1 tail. Should you automatically assume the coin to be biased? What is the explanation for your answer?

2. Are you more likely to draw a black king from a pack of playing cards or a spade of any suit? How did you determine your answer?

3. What is the probability of drawing a black playing card followed by a red playing card?

Discussion points

1. Why should you be cautious about stating an event will take place even though the probability of it happening is 99.9%?

2. Probability theory is based on an assumption of 'no bias'. Do you think that such a state of 'no bias' is possible? Support your case with examples.

Assignment

Carry out a small-scale census of traffic flow past a given landmark during, say, half an hour (if busy), or an hour (if not). Categorise vehicles by type while counting into cars, vans, goods trucks, bicycles, motorbikes, etc. Out of the total flow of traffic, work out the proportion of each category of vehicle. Repeat the exercise at the same time the next day (do this mid-week so as not to include a weekend). Compare the results from the two observations and explain how far the first day's observations were, or were not, predictive of those made on the second day.

Study tips

Venn diagrams are a very useful way of representing a probability problem. You can see relationships and work out possible event outcomes.

2

Populations and Sampling

One-minute Overview – In statistics a population has a very specific meaning. It is the total number of subjects (which are not necessarily people) of your research that conform to a clearly defined set of characteristics. You are always collecting data on a characteristic (variable) that varies within the **population**, you are assuming that there is a spread of values across this population. The theoretical spread of this quantity across the population is called the normal distribution. A number of statistical techniques assume a normal distribution of the variable concerned. If a population is very large, a sample is drawn and the results generalised to the population as a whole. To ensure confidence in the reliability of our conclusions, we use **probability sampling** to select the sample to make sure it is representative of the population as a whole. This chapter considers the nature of a population and how it may be reliably **sampled**. It covers:

▶ the nature of a population
▶ sampling a population

The nature of a population

The subjects of your study are collectively referred to as the **population.** How you define the population is extremely important. You need to be very clear about who, or what, should be included. Let's take a couple of examples.

1. Salary levels of male accountants aged 25 to 45
Here there are three very clear parameters (or conditions) that define your population. All subjects within the population will be male, accountants, and aged between 25 and 45.

2. Annual turnover of companies with fewer than 250 employees

The population for your investigation will be all companies employing fewer than 250 people. This second example shows that a population is not necessarily composed of people. You want to gather information about companies which are officially described as small to medium sized enterprises, SMEs for short.

Problems in identifying your population

In example 1 we know exactly who or what should be in our population, but example 2 is trickier. For example, do you include companies that are subsidiaries of a much larger organisation? A small company may be part of a multinational corporation and be very different from a privately owned company lacking the support of a parent organisation! In short, when identifying your population, be very precise about its exact nature and the parameters for inclusion.

Normal distribution of a variable

While your population is identified by some fixed parameter(s), you intend to look at how one or more other properties of that population varies. In example 1 above, you want to explore how salary levels are distributed amongst the population. Any property of a population that you are measuring is called a **variable.**

Figure 2.1 shows what is known as a **normal distribution** of a variable in a theoretical population. If you were to collect information about salaries of male accountants aged between 25 and 45, you would expect there to be a wide variation. The spread should, in theory at least, look something like figure 2.1, with a few at the bottom end and top end of the salary spectrum, and a large number bunched around the middle.

This theoretical shape is assumed to apply to any variable in a population. In practice, it doesn't always work out like that. Figure 2.2 shows two distribution patterns where the maximum frequency is nearer one end of the graph; in other words it shows **skew**. This can be positive or negative skew. Many statistical techniques assume that the distribution of values of a variable conforms to the normal distribution. If there is excessive skew, then you need to be cautious about using any of those techniques.

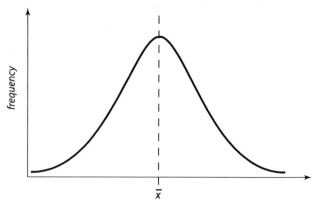

continuous variable being measured

Figure 2.1 Normal distribution of a variable in a
theoretical population.

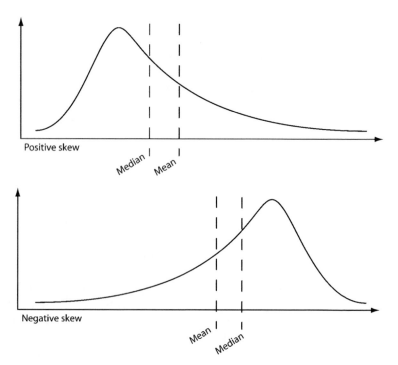

Figure 2.2 Distribution patterns showing skew.

▶ *Key point* – The key physical characteristic of a normal distribution is that it is symmetrical about the peak. The peak (the maximum occurrence or frequency) is the theoretical **mean** value (colloquially referred to as the **average** value). Half of the population falls to the left of the peak and half falls to the right of it.

Keep the idea of **normal distribution** – and its theoretical significance – firmly in mind. We will be revisiting it later in the book.

Sampling a population

In an ideal world you will collect the research data from the entire population. While this is possible where the population is small, you will not usually have the time or resources to do it. The only way around this is to select a proportion of the total population – i.e. a **sample**.

After collecting and analysing data from the sample, you will want to say that your conclusions apply to the population as a whole. But can you? There is a problem. If you choose a sample size of, say, 20% of the population, how can you be sure that any conclusions based on the analysis apply to the whole population? You have no data on 80% of the population!

You cannot be absolutely certain of being able to generalise, but there are sampling procedures that help to improve the probability of being able to do so accurately. There are two problems to address:

1. How large should a sample be?
2. Who should be in the sample?

The first problem will be described at the end of this chapter.

The sample as representative of the population

Logic suggests that, if conclusions are to be generalised to the whole population, the sample should be representative of the population in some way. The techniques used to select the sample are collectively called **probability sampling**. You will remember from chapter 1 that the probability of being selected through random selection is directly related to the proportion of subjects available to be selected.

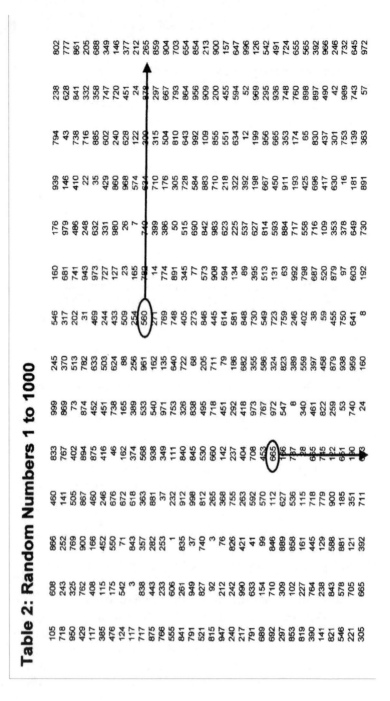

Table 2.1. A random numbers table.

Simple random sampling

Suppose you randomly select a male accountant from the population of those aged 25 to 45. The probability of selecting a 35 year-old accountant is equal to the proportion of 35 year-olds. So, if your population is 100 individuals, of whom 20 are 35 years old, there is a 20% chance of selecting one. Equally, if the proportion of 45 year-olds is 40%, then this is the probability of selecting a 45 year-old. In theory your sample will now contain accountants whose distribution of ages represents that of the population.

However, you still need to apply a system that ensures randomness, and which minimises bias. Simply listing all the names and then selecting every tenth name may look **random**, but who wrote down the list? Was it in alphabetical order, or organised in some other way, deliberately or otherwise? The accepted way of selection is by assigning a number to every individual subject of the population. A table of random numbers is used to select your sample.

Table 2.1 shows part of a table of random numbers. You can buy tables or, if you know how, use computer software, such as Microsoft Excel to generate them.

Using the random numbers table

Suppose there are 1000 subjects in your population and you have decided to take a 10% sample (i.e. 100). A list of all the subjects within the population is drawn up. This is called the **sampling frame**. Each subject in the sampling frame is given a number from 1 to 1000 that is unique to it.

The next stage is to use the table of random numbers to identify the subjects for your sample. There is no science involved here. Close your eyes and stick a pin on the page!

1. Whichever number it hits is your starting point.

2. Now work horizontally (or vertically) and record each number in the row or column. For example, in table 2.1, the number 665 has been circled. The subject identified by this number has been selected. Working downwards, the next number is 166, and so on until you reach the bottom of the column.

3. Where a number is repeated, skip it and move on to the next.

4. Having reached the bottom of the column, close your eyes and select another starting point. In our example, 560 is circled as the second starting point, and the direction is taken as horizontal.

5. The job is done when your sample of 100 has been selected.

Stratified sampling

The problem with simple random sampling lies in one of the basic difficulties of predicting the outcome of any particular random event. You might expect a randomly selected sample to be representative of the population as a whole, but it may very well not be! For example, if you wanted to compare attitudes towards professionalism of male and female accountants to see if gender was an important factor, it would be very unfortunate if your sample turned up a disproportionate number of one gender. It is theoretically possible to end up with one male and 2 999 females, which is no use at all!

To reduce the risk of this you would **stratify** the sampling. Looking at the example in the last paragraph, it is important that the sample is representative of the gender balance in the population – because this is a key factor to be researched. Your population has 30 000 subjects, of which 10 000 are female. Your sample needs to be representative of this gender balance. If a 10% sample is to be taken in other words 3000 – you will need 1000 female and 2000 male accountants.

You split your population into the strata you are trying to properly represent – in this case, gender. In effect you generate separate sampling frames for each strata. The simple random sampling method is now applied to each stratum so that 1000 female and 2000 male accountants are selected.

It is possible to use stratified probability sampling using more than one factor. For example, you may want to know if attitudes to professionalism are related to gender and/or educational level of entrants. Figure 2.3 shows how the population has been stratified into four strata.

Multi-stage cluster sampling

At first sight this may look like stratified sampling, but the similarity is skin deep. A typical scenario for this form of sampling might be a study of the victims of crime in the UK. In considering your sample, you have a number of factors to consider in order to gain a good representation of the population. For example, there is a wide

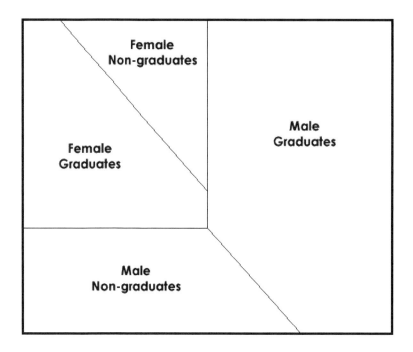

Figure 2.3. The stratification of a population.

geographical spread, a range of urban and rural settings, and a range of economic and social conditions within the local authority ward. You can't sample everyone.

Representation can be achieved by **multi-stage cluster sampling**. You use stratified sampling to select a representative sample of urban and rural local authorities across the UK. Within each of the selected authorities, you might generate a stratified sample of wards, and within each ward, you might sample roads and then individual residences. The whole process is funnelling you towards a sample that has been selected using probability sampling to ensure it is representative of the UK population as a whole. Since the sampling frame for a study of this size is huge (millions of households), this stepwise approach is an effective way of managing the research.

Opportunity sampling

This method of sampling appears to have a semblance of randomness about it. For example, interviewers may be asked to interview every tenth woman who passes them in the street. But it is more likely that the interviewers have quotas. An interviewer may have to interview a certain number of people in each of a number of age groups. However, look at this approach more closely and you will see that there is bias built in the method.

The interviewer will be standing in a busy thoroughfare, so should easily achieve the required number of interviews. Even if simple random, or multi-stage cluster sampling for that matter, has been used to identify the location of the survey, *you* are not selected at random. Bias is introduced in two ways:

1. You may have made eye contact and so were pounced upon! In other words, you become selected because the opportunity was there by virtue of your attention being attracted.

2. You are selected because you happen to be there on that day at that time and so have increased the probability of being selected. If you had decided to stay at home (or were quick to spot the interviewer and dive into a shop to avoid detection) your probability of selection would have been 0%.

Despite these flaws, the method is used very extensively in market research. It is easy to operate and is one way of sampling a population so large that a sampling frame cannot be devised. So long as it is understood that this method does not constitute probability sampling, and that the results need to be treated with caution, the method can be used to overcome the problem of an indeterminate population.

The sample size

Ideally, the entire population should be surveyed. In drawing a sample you need to be mindful of its size. Too small a sample may lead you to difficulties because its members are not as representative of the population. The question is how large a sample?

The larger the sample the more confidence you can have in your findings. This is an obvious statement to make, but it is a property of your research that may easily be forgotten in the quest to make statements about the population as a whole. When you use a sample to measure the average age of accountants you are actually calculating the average age within the sample. What you want to be able to do is to make a statement about the average age of accountants in the whole population.

There is a strong possibility that there is a real difference between the sample average age and that of the population. In other words, there will be a **sampling error**. There is a strong relationship between the sample size and the level of sampling error.

The difficulty lies in a tension between selecting a large sample, and practical cost and other constraints. The latter often loom large, and may be over-riding, so that there is a compromise between the degree of confidence in the results and the resourcing of the research. A good rule of thumb is make your sample size as large as possible.

Tutorial: helping you learn

Progress questions

1. The assignment at the end of chapter 1 asked you to sample the traffic flow past a given landmark. Explain the potential flaws in this method of sampling the total flow of traffic.

2. What is meant by the term 'population' in social science terms? How do you determine who or what should be in your research population?

3. Explain the term 'probability sampling'. Why is this approach to sampling so important in social sciences research?

Discussion point

Social scientists face a dilemma when sampling a population. In an ideal world the entire population would be included, but we can't usually do this. You want to undertake a research project to determine if there are differences in the reading ability of 10-year-olds in rural and urban schools throughout the UK. What difficulties might you face in selecting your population, and the sample you would draw from it?

Assignment

This assignment asks you to develop the research sample arising out of the discussion point above. Use an appropriate probability sampling technique to select a 20% sample of 10 year-olds in your county. Your sample should be representative of the urban and rural distribution of schools. To design this sample, you will need to determine the number, size and distribution of primary schools in your county.

Study tips

Practice is the best aid to becoming good at identifying and sampling a research population. The web site accompanying this book will give you more practice in the techniques. There are also feedback and detailed explanations to help you sort out anything you are not quite clear about. It is also a good idea to work with a partner, or at least ask someone else to look at your work. Another perspective often identifies things you have overlooked.

3

Managing Your Data

One-minute Overview – Numbers are not always what they seem. A number is a symbol, and in social statistics there are three fundamental types of numbers. A **nominal** number is used to uniquely identify a property, for example to identify a person in your database. It has no other purpose. We cannot use nominal numbers in calculations, as they have the same property as letters. It is a form of naming. **Ordinal** numbers are used for generating a sense of order, such as placing alternatives in an order of preference. Again, they cannot usually be used in calculations, but there are exceptions. **Interval** numbers represent quantities, and can be manipulated mathematically. Social surveys generate vast quantities of data and these need to be managed effectively. This is best done by computer software applications such as databases, spreadsheets and most usefully by statistics packages such as **SPSS**. In this chapter we will explore:

▶ what is a number?
▶ using computers to manage data
▶ cleaning up your database
▶ cells, records and variables

What is a number?

The notion of a number is taken for granted. You apply numbers in a range of different ways that show they have several symbolic uses.

Nominal numbers
In the last chapter we introduced the use of random number tables. We showed how to select a sample in which each member of the population was allocated a unique number to identify it. This is just like your house number, in that it uniquely identifies your property from those of your neighbours.

We can perfectly well use some other form of unique identifier, such as a letter or even words. Numbers have a very useful property: you cannot run out of them. Letters and combinations of letters, on the other hand, become cumbersome when you need to uniquely identify large quantities of individual items.

Used in this way they are referred to as **nominal**. They are used only as a means of identification. You cannot perform any arithmetical or mathematical operation on them. You cannot add two of them together to make something else. Their value in statistical analysis lies in their utility. Computer software is now the universal means of managing and manipulating statistical data, and computers find numbers easier to work with than letters or letter combinations (called **strings**). We will be looking at questionnaire design in chapter 6, and it is important to see how nominal numbers are used with them.

Questions will have a set of possible responses, or categories, and so we allocate a number, or code, to each possible response category. The following is an example.

Which method of travelling to work do you use?
(a)   train   code = 01
(b)   bus   code = 02
(c)   bicycle   code = 03
(d)   motorcycle   code = 04
(e)   your own car   code = 05
(f)   as a passenger in someone else's car   code = 06
(g)   on foot   code = 07
(h)   other (please state what this is)   code = 99

There are eight categories altogether, including 'other'. This last one is a common way of trying to capture information that you had not thought of when creating the questionnaire. It allows you to generate new codes, or to recode into one of the others if more appropriate.

Suppose a respondent chose 'other' and reported: 'None, I work from home'. You might well want to identify this as a new category, perhaps coding it 08. This is where the apparently odd numbering system comes in. In the original questionnaire there are eight categories: if new categories were discovered you would very quickly get into double figures. In that situation, you give each category a two-digit code, such as 01 etc. By coding our catch-all category 'other' as 99, you are left with plenty of room to add new codes.

Dichotomous coding

Many questions have only two possible responses. Typical of this type of question are those that require a simple 'yes' or 'no' response. Another example is the question that asks for the gender of the respondent. Even though a respondent may have changed gender at some point in life, the response will still be a definitive 'male' or 'female'. These questions are referred to as a **dichotomy**. Usually, the responses are coded as 0 and 1, or 1 and 2.

Ordinal numbers

Ordinal numbers represent order. Look at the following question:

Place each of the following colours in your order of preference, from 1st to 5th:

    red   blue   orange   green   yellow

The question asks you to order the colours. The researcher codes your response by allocating numbers 1 to 5 in descending order of preference, for example:

red	1
yellow	2
orange	3
green	4
blue	5

The order in which the options are placed then becomes the code for that category. This means that the code is not fixed. For example, 'blue' could be coded 1, 2, 3, 4 or 5 depending on how a respondent defines his or her preference.

Ordinal numbers do not represent quantity, simply an ordering. So, you cannot say that the respondent liked red twice as mush as yellow, or four times as much as green. You only know the order of preference. Again this means that no arithmetical or mathematical operations can be carried out on these numbers.

(Actually, this is not strictly true. There are certain conditions under which ordinal numbers might be treated in the same way as **interval numbers**: see below. There is some debate about this and purists will argue against it. However, those statisticians who do hold to the view that you can treat some ordinal measures as interval ones argue that the errors incurred are so small as to be unimportant. If there are a large number of ordinal categories, then they can be treated as interval.)

Typical questions that generate this type of data are **multiple-item** questions. These are designed to measure one variable through the use of a number of sub-questions, each with their own ordinal responses. Calculating the sum of the responses might create a measure of the variable. This will give a large number of possible categories. For example, the question below seeks to determine the respondent's job satisfaction by linking together a number of factors. Only the first two items have been shown, but there might be many more.

Please indicate whether you strongly disagree (1), disagree (2), are undecided (3), agree (4), or strongly agree (5) with each of the following statements. Please circle one answer only for each statement:

	Strongly disagree	Disagree	Undecided	Agree	Strongly agree
I enjoy going to work each day	1	2	3	4	5
My work is interesting to me	1	2	3	4	5

If there are ten items, each has a minimum of 1 and a maximum of 5. Calculating the sum of these ordinal scores will result in anything from 10 to 50. This represents a range of 40 possible categories for job satisfaction. You could treat this measure as an interval measure.

Interval numbers

These are numbers that actually represent quantities. They can be manipulated by arithmetical processes, so for example you can work out that your overdraft at the bank is twice as large as it was last month! As such, interval numbers are very powerful in data analysis.

A good example of this power relates to questionnaire design. Look at these two questions.

1. What age were you at your last birthday?

2. What is your age (please select your age range)?

> (Under 18, 18-25, 26-35, 36-45, 46-55, over 55.)

Question 1 allows you to say that the 18 year-old is twice the age of the 36 year-old respondent. In question 2 this is not possible because you cannot know the exact age. The answer to question 1 will be an interval number, while question 2 will be an ordinal number.

Using computers to manage data

Social surveys result in the collection of vast quantities of primary data that must be managed at all stages of its collection and analysis. By far the most sensible way of doing this is with the use of computer software.

Data collection and entry

Questionnaire data needs to be entered into a database so it can be manipulated later as part of the data analysis process. Data entry must be quick and accurate. If you have 20 000 questionnaires to process, time becomes a major issue.

Of course, speeding up data entry may come with a heavy price, namely loss of accuracy. This is a very serious problem because if you are going to make judgements on the basis of this data inaccuracies can invalidate your findings, or at the very least weaken any hypotheses you may want to put forward. Even worse, you may not even know this because the errors are unknown to you, being hidden amongst the mass of data fields within the database.

Data analysis and output

The second important function of software used in statistical analysis is that of carrying out the calculations. This could be the same software as that used for data entry. Alternatively, you might use a database package with a user-friendly data entry screen, and another package for analysing the data. If you choose this option, make sure you can 'export' the data from the database in a format that the second computer application can use.

Displaying the results

When the application has done its calculations, it needs to display the results clearly. A particularly useful – and important – feature of computers is the ability to present results graphically. They can create **graphs** and **frequency tables** that allow you to judge **distribution** and **patterns**. In other words you will be able to assess whether or not there is a normal distribution of the data for any given variable, or whether some values should be suspected of being errors.

Suitable software applications

To some extent, this section contains recommendations about software. This does not mean to say that other software packages will not do the job. Use the comments made here as a benchmark for judging their suitability. Space is too short to describe them all.

▶ *Microsoft Access* – You can design a **database** in Access. You can set up a data entry form to make it easier to enter the data. You can help reduce errors by specifying what may or may not be accepted by any one data field. For example, if the coding only allows 1, 2 and 3, an accidental entry of 5 will be rejected. However, this will not prevent an incorrect data entry of, say, 1 when it should have been 2. Still, it helps, because a data entry error is quite often the result of entering data out of order. Figure 3.1 shows a database table being set up, and figure 3.2 shows the data entry form it creates.

▶ *Microsoft Excel* - Excel is a **spreadsheet** application, that lends itself to a wide range of other uses. Once you have set up the spreadsheet to receive the data, a **form** can be used to enter the data. Figure 3.3 shows a data entry form with its spreadsheet. However, this is not

Variable Name

Data Type

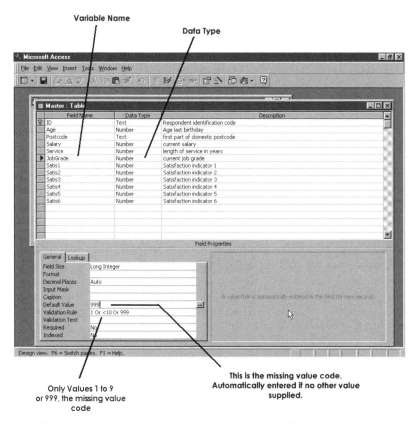

**Only Values 1 to 9
or 999, the missing value
code**

**This is the missing value code.
Automatically entered if no other value
supplied.**

Figure 3.1. A database table being set up in MicroSoft Access.

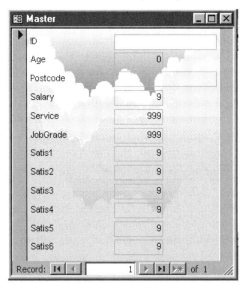

Figure 3.2. A data entry form in MicroSoft Access.

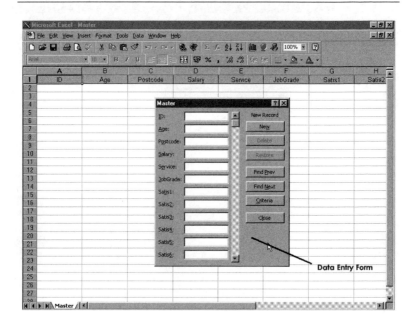

Figure 3.3. A data entry form with its spreadsheet.

as user-friendly as Access. However, where Excel does have the edge over Access is in data analysis. You can use the 'Function' facility, or the 'Data analysis' option in the 'Tools' menu, to carry out statistical operations on the data.

One way to work with data is to use Access for setting up a database and entering data, and then 'export' the complete database as an Excel file for data analysis in the spreadsheet.

SPSS (Statistics Package for the Social Sciences)
By far the best way to work with data is with software packages designed for the purpose you want. SPSS is one of the best known and widely used software packages for the statistical analysis of social data. However, the data editor window (the screen for entering and editing the data) is not very user-friendly, as it looks just like a spreadsheet. SPSS can import data from a variety of other software applications, including Excel and other databases. You could use other packages for data entry and then import into SPSS for the data analysis.

The real power of SPSS lies in the ability it gives you to interact

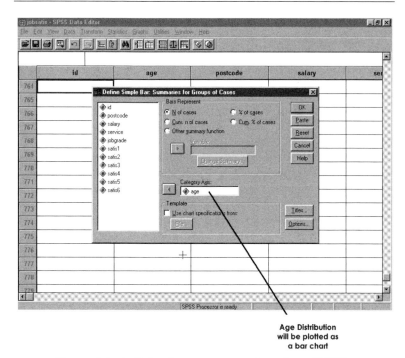

**Age Distribution
will be plotted as
a bar chart**

Figure 3.4. A dialog box to create a bar chart (SPSS).

with the software, so you can manipulate the data with great precision. SPSS has its own scripting language, and expert users can type in instructions (like mini-programs) to meet individual analytical needs. However, since you are probably not an expert user, each analytical operation can be controlled using dialog boxes. These prompt you to specify what you want. Figure 3.4 for example shows a dialog box to create a bar chart.

A really useful facility of the current version of SPSS is the ability to export the results of your analysis into a format that you can insert directly into a word-processed report, or even an internet web site.

Cleaning up your database

It is almost inevitable that a few errors will creep in when entering the data no matter how careful you are. The first job after data entry is to check for accuracy. This is tedious with large data sets, but it is an essential routine.

There are a couple of methods you can use to visually check for errors or inconsistencies:

1. Print out the entire data set, if it is not too large. Check each case individually against the actual questionnaire.

2. If the data set is large, print out a table listing of each variable individually showing the frequency of each code. This will show up codes that shouldn't be there. For example, if the possible codes are 1, 2 and 3, any other numbers are obviously errors.

The question now arises as to how you should deal with errors. If you know what the correct response should be then you may make a correction.

▶ *Key point* – If the correct response is unknown (perhaps you cannot identify the questionnaire for that case) then there is an ethical issue. *Do not guess the response.* Treat is as though the respondent did not respond to the question and leave it blank. The reason is that, if you make a decision about what you believe the respondent actually recorded, you are falsifying the data, and this is unacceptable.

SPSS allows you to account for this by making an obvious error a **missing value**. The program will then ignore this case when making its calculations. The output from these calculations will show that there were missing values, and how many, so you can make a decision about the reliability of the outcome.

Cells, records, and variables

These terms are commonly used in any work using databases. It will pay you to become familiar with the terms, and so they are defined here. Refer also to figure 3.5 for a pictorial representation.

Cells
Your database is made up of a **matrix** of cells, or individual items of

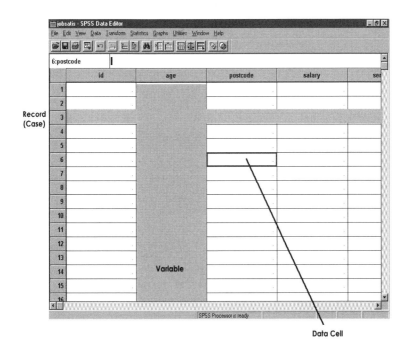

Figure 3.5. A pictorial representation of a database.

data. When you enter information, such as the respondent's age, it is entered into the matrix to form one cell of data.

Records

A horizontal row of cells will hold the data collected from one respondent. In other words, it is a **record** of one **case**. Each respondent is referred to as a case.

Variables

This was defined in chapter 2 as the property or characteristic about which you are collecting data. Therefore, age may be a variable, gender may be another, and annual salary might be a third. In a database, a vertical column of cells will hold the data on a single variable gathered from all the cases in the study.

Tutorial: helping you learn

Progress questions

1. Explain what is meant by the terminology **nominal**, **ordinal** and **interval** numbers. Give examples of each that might be used in a social statistics context.

2. Why would a social researcher use the following codes for the response categories of a question?

prefer to walk	code = 1
prefer private transport	code = 2
prefer public transport	code = 3
other	code = 9

3. If you were considering what computer software package to use for data management, what would you need to take into account?

Discussion points

1. You have been asked to undertake a social survey of student attitudes towards work. The sample size is 2000. Discuss the data management issues associated with such a large survey.

2. What computer software packages are available for use? Discuss which ones you will use for this survey. What will be the likely merits and disadvantages associated with your choice?

Assignment

Create a database from the dataset provided on the books website. Go to the Chapter 3 page, where you will find the data under Assignment. Use the most appropriate computer program you have available to you. Check your database for errors against the original data. You will be using this database for other exercises in the book so this assignment is unavoidable!

Study tips

At every opportunity, examine questionnaires to see how the response categories are formulated. Sometimes they will also show the codes used for each response. Determine what type of code they use (nominal, ordinal or interval).

4

Research Questions, Concepts and Operationalisation

One-minute Overview – All research requires you to be very clear about your **research questions**. These help you to identify the main issues, and to remain focused. The research question may be developed from a **hypothesis** you want to test. As you develop your question you will identify **concepts** – ideas that help us interpret and make sense of the world. These concepts will need to be **operationalised** – expressed in a way to help us create measurable indicators of the concepts. Once a concept has been operationalised, you can design the questions to collect the data needed to measure it. For example, you need to have an operational definition of 'work' before you can create questions to ask people about their work. Only then will you be able to identify and explore differences between people. In this chapter we will explore:

▶ the hypothesis
▶ operationalising a concept
▶ selecting measurable indicators
▶ refining your research question

The hypothesis

Most social research is about 'hypothesis building' or 'testing'. You need to begin your research with a very specific target in mind.

▶ *A hypothesis* – is a working assumption. For example: 'The employment patterns of women in rural communities is generally different to those of women in urban communities.'

A hypothesis does not need to have any basis in fact. It is simply an idea you want to test. By looking at the data, you will be able to confirm or deny the assertion. So a hypothesis is a preliminary assertion you want to test. However, before you can begin to collect the data that will test your hypothesis, you need to prepare your research questions.

The research questions

Before you can collect data, you will need a very clear specification of the issue being researched – the research question. Specifying this is not quite as easy as it might sound. For example, suppose you want to find out what 'work' people do. There are some questions you, as the researcher, will need to clarify. For example:

1. What do you mean by work?

2. Who will be the subjects of this study, and where are they?

3. Over what time period? work patterns may change.

The second and third questions are fairly straightforward. The sampling approach described in chapter 2 will take care of question 2. For question 3 a decision needs to be made about what is wanted. If it is to be a 'snapshot' view taken at a particular point in time, it is an easy matter to specify a date in your questions.

If, on the other hand, you are investigating potential changes in the pattern of work, you might want to make regular surveys of your subjects' work at given dates over a time period or cycle (e.g. December 31st, March 31st, June 30th and September 30th). You would need to carry out this survey over a long period of time (say several years) to establish any pattern.

To continue with this example, your research question might be:

> Are there any differences in the work pattern of women compared with men in the small rural community of XXX?

You can identify the population and use sampling theory to produce your sample, but you are left with a fundamental problem to solve before you can proceed with the development of a questionnaire. You have a **concept** that needs to be clearly understood and defined and that is the meaning of 'work', question 1 in the list.

Defining a concept

A concept is an idea that we use to make sense of the world. It is an interpretation or description of what we observe.

▶ *Example* – Gender is a concept. It is based on our understanding of maleness and femaleness.

Age is another concept, as is 'poverty', 'job satisfaction', 'power' and 'unemployment'. As you read this paragraph, you will have an understanding of these terms, but that is where the potential problem lies. Your understanding of the concepts may differ from that of another reader. In the social sciences, this creates difficulties if you try to measure them. If there are differences between researchers' understanding of these concepts, there can be no guarantee that two pieces of research on the subject are comparing like with like.

Common sense meanings

There is often a common sense meaning associated with a concept. For example, if you ask people in the street what they understand by the term 'work' there is likely to be broad agreement. However, there will also be some differences in understanding.

▶ *Example* – Some people will regard unpaid charity work as 'real' work while others will not. This broad understanding is not enough for social research that needs to collect data to build or test hypotheses as described in chapter 9. There needs to be a common understanding of a concept.

Before collecting data via questionnaires or other means you need to have a clear idea of what it is you are collecting data on. This seems obvious, but this important point is often overlooked or not properly thought through.

The natural sciences get around this problem by providing very specific and unambiguous definitions. In the social sciences this is often more difficult: many of the concepts are very abstract, and not the result of detailed experiment and mathematical testing.

Hard-to-define concepts

While many concepts have a generally accepted definition, others are much more difficult because there is no universally agreed under-standing. For example, 'power' will often mean different things to different people. Also, 'leadership' will generate an interesting debate about its meaning. How do concepts like 'social class' or 'poverty' measure up in terms of a shared understanding?

It is not always important to have a universally agreed definition of a particular social concept. So long as you have a very clear and precise definition of the particular concept you are investigating, and this definition is clearly communicated to others, there can be a common understanding of the concept in your terms. However, some concepts do need to have a universal definition, otherwise one cannot establish consistent methods of measurement and comparison. For example, without a common definition of 'unemployment' it would be difficult to compare employment statistics across the different areas of the UK or Europe.

The same goes for any concept that is going to be used to determine social policy. These concepts could include 'poverty', 'deprivation', 'productivity', and a host of others that researchers and government departments wish to measure. Psychology, too, requires a common understanding of concepts such as 'intelligence' or 'aptitude', otherwise it becomes impossible to compare different psychological tests that measure them.

Importance of consistency
Consistency is also important for comparing changes over time ('longitudinal studies'). If we want to see how social policy affects the labour market, then we need a universally accepted definition of 'unemployment' to develop a way of measuring it across geographical regions and over time.

A clear definition is the first stage in creating a means of exploring and measuring a concept. Developing the means of measuring a concept is called 'operationalisation'.

Operationalising a concept

Figure 4.1 shows the process of 'operationalisation'. Chapters 5 and 6 look at how to put together questions and questionnaires that will collect the data you need for a social research project.

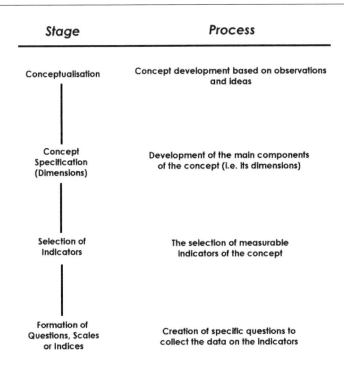

Figure 4.1. The process of 'operationalising' a concept.

Conceptualisation

Here you formulate the concept in broad terms based on observations, ideas and discussions with others. For example, you may formulate a concept of 'work'. This might be based on what you observe people doing, or what they say they do. Of course, there is the physical science definition of work to contend with as well. Is there a relationship between the two? So we might say, 'Work is activity that we must undertake in order to satisfy our physical and social needs.' This is probably not an entirely satisfactory description of the concept, but let's stick with it for the purpose of this chapter.

Concept specification

Now that we have defined a concept of 'work', the next stage is to identify the components ('dimensions') of work. Much thought and observation should be devoted to examining and clarifying the dimensions of a concept. This will include looking at other research on the subject: how have others defined the dimensions of 'work'?

At the end of this process, you should come up with a list of dimensions that constitute 'work'. For example your list could include:

1. an activity for which the individual receives payment from another individual or organisation

2. an activity required to maintain the family and home

3. an activity that is unpaid but undertaken for the benefit of other members of society

4. an activity that *must* be carried out, rather than one pursued purely for pleasure (NB: We do need to recognise that work can be pleasurable as well as necessary, but activity that is only for pleasure is not being classified as work here).

You can probably think of other dimensions of 'work', but at this stage we are keeping the idea simple so as to develop the argument.

The development of concept 'dimensions' is important for two reasons. Firstly, it clearly defines the concept in concrete terms that can be universally understood. Secondly, it provides you with a means of being able to develop indicators to measure the nature of work.

Selecting measurable indicators

The next stage is to identify measurable indicators for each dimension. Continuing with the concept of 'work', three hypothetical dimensions were identified in the last section.

Example dimensions of 'work'
Paid work
The measurable indicator for this dimension is whether or not payment is received for work carried out.

Home and family
There may be a number of indicators relating to work required to maintain home and family. For example:

1. housework
2. DIY and home maintenance
3. caring for dependants.

Volunteering

You might want to determine memberships of voluntary organisations and any activities the individual is involved with. Here the activity could be classified as 'work' because it is for the benefit of other members of society.

Duration

Of course, not everyone does the same amount of work in a day, week or month. Also, if work can be identified through a variety of dimensions as described above, an individual may do more than one type of work. In this case, how much time is devoted to each?

Summary

We find that 'work' turns out to be a complex concept, one we cannot fully describe in a single sentence. Only after going through this process of 'operationalisation' will you be able to design questions to measure an individual's involvement with work, and hence determine and explore differences between people – the essence of social research.

Refining your research question

As you work through the operationalising of concepts for your research question, you will often need to refine it so that it takes account of their complexities. In other words, you will need to become more precise about what you are exploring, or to be able to tackle the question in manageable bits.

A series of additional specific questions may arise as a result of you considering the concept of *work*. These are called 'corollary questions'. Your research question may now look something like this:

Are there any differences in the work pattern of women compared with men in the small rural community of **XXX**?

1. Are there differences in patterns during the year (e.g. seasonal)?
2. Are there differences between age groups?
3. Are there differences in the type of work and amount of time spent?

The initial idea was to research the possible differences in work patterns between genders, and to operationalise the concepts within the question. Now, you are arriving at a refined research question and a set of measurable indicators. These indicators need to be converted into questions that can be used to collect the necessary data. We will come to this in chapter 6.

A final point to remember about the research question, is that it has a very practical use – apart from the obvious one of telling everyone what you are researching. As you move deeper into your research, you will risk getting bogged down with detail and the sheer mass of data you collect. It will be easy to become side-tracked from your original purpose. Going back to look at the research question from time to time will help to keep you focused.

Tutorial: helping you learn

Progress questions
1. What is a hypothesis?

2. What is the main purpose of research questions?

3. What is meant by the term concept in social research?

4. What name is given to the process of creating measurable indicators from a concept? Why is this process so important?

Discussion points
Either on your own, or preferably with two or three other people, examine the concept of 'social class'. Try to reach an agreement about what it means and identify what you think are its principal dimensions. What difficulties does this present you with?

Assignment
Prepare research questions to help you design research, that will test the hypothesis: 'men gain greater job satisfaction than women'. You will need to identify the concepts involved, operationalise them, and identify measurable indicators. Don't forget, you can use current social science literature to help you; the concept of job satisfaction has been widely written about.

Study tips

1. It is a good idea to familiarise yourself with some of the major concepts in the social sciences and gain a clear understanding of what they mean.

2. Keep abreast of the current literature in an area of particular interest to you or the areas you are focusing on in your course.

3. Academic papers usually contain an introductory section that examines the concepts under investigation, and looks at its definitions and dimensions. Remember to do the same when you are writing reports and assignments for your course. Make sure there is a common understanding of the concepts you are exploring in your work.

Indices and Scales

One-minute Overview – An **index** is a useful way of comparing values over time or across geographical areas or social groupings. Actual quantities are not needed, so the problem of dealing with large cumbersome numbers is eliminated. An index represents a value as a proportion of another (effectively as a percentage). A **scale** is a means of measuring differences between individuals. For example, a scale may measure differences in attitudes towards a concept. **Likert** scales do this very effectively by asking respondents to indicate their level of agreement with statements. **Semantic differentials** require respondents to indicate their reaction to bi-polar descriptors (e.g. good/bad) that places them on a continuum from one extreme to the other. **Ratings** enable the researcher to measure a respondent's perception of the quality of experience; **ranking** gains a respondent's views on the relative importance of individual statements within a group of statements. In this chapter we will explore:

▶ indices
▶ scales
▶ the semantic differential
▶ rating and ranking

Indices

An index represents one value as a proportion of another. Indices are often used where a standardised means of comparing values is needed. It is particularly useful for comparing changes over a period of time, and for showing differences between individual subjects of your study (e.g. people or geographical regions). Table 5.1 shows an example of an index.

The table summarizes a number of key economic statistics comparing the data on the EU states in 2003. The final column is

Economic Statistics, 2003		
	People in employment (thousands)	Gross domestic product per head EUR 25 = 100, 2002
EUR 25	193,221	100.0
Austria	3,736	120.8
Belgium	4,070	116.8
Cyprus	327	82.9
Czech Republic	4,701	67.6
Denmark	2,707	122.5
Estonia	594	46.6
Finland	2,365	113.8
France	24,584	113.0
Germany	35,927	108.7
Greece	4,274	77.6
Hungary	3,922	58.6
Ireland	1,797	132.7
Italy	22,054	109.0
Latvia	1,007	39.0
Lithuania	1,433	42.4
Luxembourg	188	212.7
Malta	148	73.2
Netherlands	8,121	122.1
Poland	13,617	45.6
Portugal	5,118	76.7
Slovakia	2,162	51.3
Slovenia	897	75.3
Spain	16,695	94.6
Sweden	4,314	114.8
United Kingdom	28,696	117.8

Table 5.1: Economic statistics 2003
(*Source: Eurostat; Office for National Statistics*)

an *index* and provides a way of comparing performance in a standardized way that is based on proportion rather than a direct comparison of raw values.

The index compares the Gross Domestic Product (GDP) per head of population. Clearly the population of states varies and so the use of an *index* makes the comparison independent of numbers. An *index* requires the use of a base value and in this case, this is taken as the mean GDP of all EU states – this is recorded as 100. In effect, the index represents a percentage of the base value and provides a visual comparative measure – in this case a measure of relative national wealth. From this table it can be seen that in 2003, Latvia has the lowest national wealth at 39% of the EU average, and Luxembourg the highest at 212.7% of the EU average.

Creating an Index

Creating an *index* is a straightforward percentages calculation, but some thought is needed to identify its purpose. What are you comparing? There can be much debate around this area of index construction, especially where social policy is concerned. The consumer price index (CPI), for example, is a measure of consumer spending, and this value is compared with the value twelve months ago. If the value of average consumer spending in July 2007 was £756 and its value in July 2006 was £740 the CPI would have been:

$$CPI = \left(\frac{\text{Value in 2007}}{\text{Value in 2006}} \right) \times 100\%$$

$$CPI = \left(\frac{756}{740} \right) \times 100 = 102.2$$

This would make the annual inflation rate in July 2007 as 2.2%.

The general calculation for creating an index is:

$$\text{Index} = \frac{\text{Value to compare}}{\text{Base value}} \times 100$$

Indices are interval measures.

Weighting an index

An *index* based purely on raw values of its components can present

	UK (2007 = 100)		Seaside town	
age group	% age group*	mean income	% age group*	mean income
16 – 44	42	£350	30	£300
45 – 59	20	£400	25	£350
60 – 79	14	£185	30	£200
80 +	4	£160	10	£200

Table 5.2. Hypothetical data on mean incomes for the UK
and a seaside town.
(*Note: Under-16s have been excluded, so the % does not total 100%.)

some difficulties because it does not show the relative influence of each component. Suppose you want to create an index of individual income as a measure of personal affluence. The problem you face when comparing different areas will be their population structure. In general, retired people tend to have a lower income than younger working people. Also, people in their late 30s, 40s and 50s generally have higher incomes than those in their early 20s. In other words, there can be influences on the income that you will want to 'control' for.

You can **weight** the index so that like is compared with like, so no matter what the age group composition of an area you can make a comparison that is independent of this potential bias. Table 5.2 shows hypothetical data on mean incomes for the UK and a seaside town on the south coast.

There are two features of note. The seaside town has a higher proportion of elderly people who appear more affluent than the hypothetical UK elderly population. It also has an under-60 population that appears to be less affluent than the hypothetical UK population. An index based on the mean of means using the UK as the base is calculated as follows:

$$\text{income index} = \frac{\text{mean of UK means}}{\text{mean of seaside town means}} \times 100$$

$$\text{income index} = (262.5/273.75) \times 100 = 95.9$$

		UK (2007 = 100)		Seaside town	
age group	% age group	mean income	weighted aggregate*	mean income	weighted aggregate*
16 – 44	42	£350	£14,700	£300	£12,600
45 – 59	20	£400	£8,000	£350	£7,500
60 – 79	14	£185	£2,590	£200	£2,800
80 +	4	£160	£640	£200	£800
		Totals	£25,930		£23,700

Table 5.3. Age adjusted index.
(*Note: – % age group x mean income.)

In other words, the population of the seaside town appears to be less affluent than the UK population as a whole. This is fine as far as it goes, but there could be difficulties later when trying to make comparisons over time. For example, how can you tell that changes are due to real changes in income, or to changes in the age distribution of the population?

You can overcome this by standardising the age distribution. Make your calculation assuming the UK age group distribution for the seaside town. Table 5.3 shows this.

Adjusted income index = (23,700/25,900) x 100 = 89.5

The new figure reduces the impact of the affluent elderly population that has distorted the picture, and plays up the effect of the younger population in keeping with the rest of the UK. This difference is quite important: the way age groups spend or save their income is often quite different.

Changing the index base

You will sometimes need to change the base of your index to make new comparisons. Table 5.4 is a hypothetical table of indices used by a company to calculate special bonuses. It takes 2000 as its base. Suppose the company decided to revise this scheme in 2003, because

Year	Value of old index (2000 = 100)	Value of new index (2003 = 100)
2000	100	105.3
2001	95	100.0
2002	90	94.7
2003	95	100.0
2004	102	107.4
2005	110	115.8
2006	115	121.0
2007	132	138.9
2008	130	136.8
2009	140	147.4

Table 5.4. Recalculating indices with a new base.

of new working practices; future bonuses will be calculated from the index using the 2003 value as its base. The indices would have to be recalculated. The table shows the old and new index values. The new value for 2000 would be calculated like this:

$$\text{new index} = \frac{\text{old index value}}{\text{new base}} \times 100$$

$$= (100/95) \times 100 = 105.3$$

Scales

You may want to measure the strength of a respondent's views on matters of interest, opinions or attitudes. You can use a scale to differentiate between respondents, so that it is possible to say respondent 'A' feels more strongly about subject 'X' than respondent 'B' does.

▶ *Key point* – A scale is an **ordinal** measure. In theory, therefore, it should not be subjected to statistical techniques that assume **interval** measures and **normal distribution** of data. However, there is an exception, when the scale scores are aggregated. This will be described a little later.

Likert scales

A Likert scale is most commonly used to measure respondents' attitudes. A question would be in the form of a statement to which respondents are asked to state their level of agreement. For example, the following question asks respondents to indicate their level of agreement with a statement about professional development and training by ticking the relevant box:

I believe it is important to keep my skills and knowledge up to date.

☐	Strongly agree	☐	Agree	☐	Not sure
☐	Disagree	☐	Strongly disagree		

The responses are coded 1 to 5 with 1 for 'strongly disagree'. The five-point scale is important, since it allows for a neutral response. A three-point scale (i.e. agree, not sure, disagree) would do. However, you would be less able to say something about the strength of agreement or disagreement, and so it is not as sensitive a measure.

However, to create a scale, you need to identify a number of attitudinal statements that reflect a particular factor you are investigating. You can then generate an aggregate score for each individual.

For example – continuing the theme of worker attitudes to continuing professional development – the following looks at some of the items that you could incorporate into a scale:

	Strongly agree	Agree	Not sure	Disagree	Strongly disagree
I believe it is important to keep my skills and knowledge up to date					
If I find that my knowledge and skills need updating, I request training					
I belive it is my employer's responsibility to identify my training needs, not mine					

Question 3 can be regarded as a negative item: agreement may seem to imply a negative attitude by denying personal responsibility. In this case, the coding would be reversed to reflect the need to score positive attitudes highly. In other words, 'Strongly agree' would be coded as 1 and 'Strongly disagree' coded as 5.

Each respondent's score is obtained by totalling the scores for each item. For example, the maximum score on the three questions above would be 15, with 3 as the minimum. There is, therefore a 12-point range of scores along which each respondent may lie. The aim is to differentiate between individual attitudes towards professional development. The more items there are in a scale, the greater the range of scores and so the more discriminating the scale will become.

Chapters 9, 10 and 11 will look at other ways of analysing data in an attempt to identify relationships. Under these circumstances it is possible to treat a scale as an **interval** measure.

If you plan to construct a scale for use on many occasions, make sure that it will discriminate between individual respondents.

Discriminative power (DP) of a Likert scale item

The ability of a scale to differentiate between individuals, by creating a wide range of scores along which your respondents are distributed, is referred to as its **discriminative power**, or DP for short. If the range of scores is relatively narrow, respondents will tend to cluster on the scale. This will make it ineffective because you won't easily be able to differentiate between individuals.

The process of constructing a scale, based on good DP, is as follows:

1. Devise as many items as you can that could be used to test a respondent's attitude to the subject under consideration (e.g. attitude to professional development).

2. Pilot the items by administering them all to a sample of people drawn using probability sampling (see chapter 2).

3. Score each respondent's responses.

4. Calculate the DP of each question.

5. Construct the scale using items with the highest DP values.

	Number of respondents	Frequency of scores					Weighted aggregate	Weighted mean
		1	2	3	4	5		
1st quartile	18	0	2	4	6	6	70	3.9
4th quartile	18	2	16	0	0	0	34	1.9

Table 5.5. Calculating the discriminative power of a Likert scale.

The DP for each question is calculated by taking the highest 25% of scores, and the lowest 25% of scores (first and lowest quartiles), to firstly determine mean score in each of the two quartiles. You then calculate the DP by subtracting the two means. The greater the difference (i.e. the higher the DP) the more effective it will be as a measure. Table 5.5 shows a hypothetical example of this type of calculation:

The DP of this scale item is 3.9 ¯ 1.9 = 2.

The semantic differential

At first sight, this scale may look like a Likert scale, but there is a fundamental difference. While you will be asking respondents to record their reactions, it is based on their reactions to a concept using a bi-polar scale. This is quite a good way of obtaining a rating of a particular concept or activity. The two ends of the scale item use contrasting adjectives. A Likert scale item only asks for the degree of agreement with a statement, but the **semantic differential** presents a continuum and asks respondents to place themselves on that continuum.

Here is a simple example of a semantic differential item:

	very	fairly	slightly	neither	slightly	fairly	very	
good								bad

Respondents will record their reactions ranging from very good to very bad. A semantic differential will provide you with rich descriptive data on any particular activity or object. The responses are coded using a 7-point scale, with 1 and 7 representing the opposite ends of the continuum, and 4 representing the neutral position.

Below is a hypothetical example of a semantic differential in which respondents are asked to provide their reactions to descriptions of MPs:

Here is a list of pairs of words that could be used to describe Members of Parliament. Between each pair is a set of boxes. Taking the first pair of words 'Truthful / Untruthful', the box on the extreme left means that you believe MPs are very truthful, while the box at the far right means that you believe MPs are very untruthful. Taking each pair in turn, please tick the box that best describes your view of MPs.

	very	fairly	slightly	neither	slightly	fairly	very	
truthful								un-truthful
hard-working								lazy
well-informed								ill-informed

Rating and ranking

▶ *Rating questions* – generate information about the quality of a respondent's experience of an event, activity or concept.

▶ *Ranking* questions – generate information about a respondent's view on the relative importance of items in a list.

Rating questions

The use of *rating* questions is very common in evaluation questionnaires, or market research. A rating response is an ordinal measure because you cannot quantify *Good* or *Very good*, for example. A hypothetical example of a rating question is given below:

Please rate the quality of the service you received by placing a tick in the appropriate box for each of the factors listed. For example, if you rate the quality of the nursing care as very good, tick the 'Very good' box.

	very good	good	satis-factory	bad	poor
quality of the nursing care					
willingness of the medical staff to listen to my concerns					
the information given to me about what my operation involved					

Each of the responses may be coded 1 (for poor) to 5 (for very good).

Ranking questions

Many concepts in social science cannot be quantified – even at the very good to poor level of rating but we can still determine the level of importance as far as an individual respondent is concerned. During analysis later, we may be able to find patterns of ordering among sub-groups of respondents.

Here is an example of a ranking question:

The three statements below refer to lifestyle characteristics that people consider important for their family. Please examine all three statements and decide which *one* is most important to you. Circle the figure 1 next to the statement. Circle the figure 3 against the statement that is least important to you. Circle the figure 2 against the remaining statement.

A high family income.	1	2	3
Time spent together in family activities.	1	2	3
My career ambitions.	1	2	3

An important feature of ranking questions is the element of forced choice. The respondent is being asked to think very carefully about what is important and then make choices about relative importance. Unlike scales and ratings, it is not possible to have the same response for each item. While very useful, these questions are often very hard for a respondent who may find some conflict between competing alternatives! For example, a high family income may be very important because it represents financial security, but the respondent has to consider if that is more important than spending time with the family. The relative order of a respondent's choice may help to explain behaviour and attitudes.

Tutorial: helping you learn

Progress questions
1. Why would you use an index to compare the relative affluence of various places in the UK?
2. What kind of information are Likert scales good at collecting?

3. Which type of question would be good at finding out the relative importance of a set of items covering judgements about what constituted a 'good life', a rating question or a ranking question?

4. What type of information is a semantic differential good at collecting?

Discussion points
In chapter 4, the assignment asked you to 'operationalise' the concept of job satisfaction and to develop measurable dimensions of the concept. Consider each of these dimensions and discuss which ones could be measured using the methods described in this chapter.

Assignment
▶ *Tip* – This assignment is best done as a group so that you can pool ideas, however, you can work alone, but there will be less learning from any debate that arises from group work.

The assignment at the end of chapter 4 asked you to look at job satisfaction and to 'operationalise' it. Take the ideas that developed from that and from the discussion above, or revisit the assignment if you have not tackled it. Then create (a) a Likert scale, (b) a semantic differential, (c) a rating scale, and (d) a ranking question that captures information about the concept dimensions you identified in the chapter 4 assignment.

Study tips
1. Other people's questionnaires are useful sources of guidance on how to use the methods described in this chapter. However, they

are not always the best examples. Look at how scales, semantic differentials, ratings and rankings have been used, but be critically aware of their use. Assess the extent to which they appear likely to be successful.

2. Official government statistics are a good example of how indices are used. Digests of such information are to be found in reference libraries. The three most useful sources of official statistics are: the Office for National Statistics (www.statistics.gov.uk); Nomis – UK labour market data (www.nomisweb.co.uk); and Eurostat – source of European Union statistics (http://epp.eurostat.ec.europa.eu).The appendices of these publications tell you how the indices have been calculated, including any weighting and adjustments. Look out for the *Annual Abstract of Statistics, Regional Trends, General Household Survey*, and *Labour Force Survey*.

6

Questionnaire Design

One-minute Overview – Most data used in statistical analysis is collected via questionnaires. This chapter looks at how to construct a questionnaire to help you collect *reliable* (consistent) data and *valid* data that measures the concepts it is meant to measure. This is achieved by carefully considering question structure and wording (e.g. closed and open responses), and the sequencing of questions (e.g. funnel, inverted funnel, filters). The pitfalls in design include inappropriate wording and language, the inclusion of leading or threatening questions, and questions that are actually asking two questions. The order of questions in the questionnaire can help to motivate a respondent to answer, or cause them to refuse. A postal questionnaire should go out with a covering letter to encourage the reader to respond. Finally, you should pilot the draft questionnaire to test that it works in the way you intended. In this chapter we will explore:

▶ reliability and validity
▶ structuring the questions
▶ structuring the questionnaire
▶ pitfalls with questionnaires
▶ the covering letter
▶ piloting the questionnaire

Reliability and validity

Where quantitative data is collected via questionnaires, great care needs to be taken to make sure the process is as free from bias as possible. The research needs to be both *reliable* and *valid*.

Reliability
The data collected, and by implication the questionnaire, is reliable if the responses to the questions are consistent.
▶ *Example* – If the questionnaire is given to a randomly selected

sample of individuals, and their responses compared with those provided by another sample selected in exactly the same way, you would hope that the results would be similar. If they are, the questionnaire is generating reliable data. Reliability is a measure of its repeatability. This particular test of reliability is called **test-retest reliability**.

Unfortunately, you will not usually be able to test your questionnaire because of the time and expense of carrying out parallel surveys. Reliability can be assessed to some extent by carrying out a pilot of your questionnaire. This is explained towards the end of the chapter. Various studies have shown that the wording of questions, the structure of the questionnaire, and the way a questionnaire is introduced to potential respondents, can all affect the responses. It can also affect a respondent's willingness to respond.

Other tests are available, but they lie outside the scope of this book.

Validity

Validity means the ability of your questionnaire to gather information on the concepts it claims to be measuring. This is a complex issue, linked to the subject content of chapter 4. For example, if you have operationalised the concept of 'job satisfaction' by identifying its dimensions, you will then construct questions to measure the concept. The validity of your questionnaire will depend on:

1. An accurate operationalisation of the concept. In other words, have you described the dimensions of the concept accurately?

2. The structure of the questions and the questionnaire are such that respondents understand what you are asking, and there are no ambiguities in wording or structure.

It is possible to design a questionnaire that is reliable because the responses are consistent, but it may be invalid because it fails to measure the concept you think it is measuring. Reliability is not a measure of validity. Again, it is beyond the scope of this book to go into detailed discussion on how to test for validity, but here are a couple of practical tips to help you at least carry out a simple assessment.

(a) If you have developed a scale, rating or ranking question, discuss its structure with others who know about the particular concept. See if they recognise and agree with your analysis.

(b) Test the question on a few people who you would expect to score highly, and on a few from whom you would expect a low score.

This is not a guarantee, but obvious errors should be identified. Testing a questionnaire for reliability and validity is both time-consuming and expensive. It usually involves large-scale piloting and comparisons with other questionnaires known to be reliable and valid.

However, what this description does tell you is that when it comes to looking at other researchers' data, you also need to ensure that their methods were valid and reliable.

Structuring the questions

The type of response required of each question can affect the way a respondent answers it. If a respondent cannot understand the question, or finds it difficult to take it seriously, there may be no response. Alternatively, you may find sarcastic or other derogatory comments written in. With the best will in the world, you will always find at least one respondent who adds comments to your questionnaire because they did not like a question or preferred to provide a response of their own!

Open or closed responses?

You are going to require one of two forms of response open or closed. A closed response question provides data that are easily coded for entering into a database, whereas an open response can often be very difficult to code. The examples given below illustrate the difference between the two.

Closed response
A typical example of this type of question might be:

From the list below, tick the <u>one</u> item that best describes the most important reason for enjoying your work

	✓	
I enjoy the variety of work		*(1)*
The working hours suit my circumstances		*(2)*
The salary is good		*(3)*
Other reason (please state reason below)		*(99)*

Each option will be given a code and this makes the job of data entry much easier. Note the 'Other reason' option. This can be a useful device to create new coded categories that you had not originally thought of. This is coded 99 to allow you to create new codes from 4 to 98 (if needed). You would do this by looking at all the responses to this question to see if there are any reasons that are repeated sufficiently often to justify a separate code.

Open response
This approach is useful if you do not wish to impose categories of response. It is also useful if you are on a 'fishing trip' to identify possible categories where you have no clear idea of what they should be. Using the question in the last section, the following might be the *open response* version of it.

> In the space below, please give one reason that best describes why you enjoy your work.

This allows respondents much greater control over what they can report.

1. The advantage of this approach is that the information will be richer and more informative than imposed categories that may not quite match up to respondents' actual experience.
2. The disadvantage is that it could present you with a coding

nightmare. Each response will need to be looked at and a category created.

An alternative, and more practical, approach is to look at common areas and create coded categories that encompass all the responses. Whatever approach you take, open response questions should be used sparingly. They take a great deal of work to analyse later.

Single or multiple response?

The two previous examples are called **single response** questions because the respondent can only choose one item. The question types discussed in chapter 5 are good examples of **multiple response** questions where respondents are asked to provide more than one response to the question asked. The use of scales, ratings and rankings require the respondent to respond to every item, but there are other ways of using a multiple response question. For example:

> From the list below choose <u>up to three</u> reasons that most influenced your choice of university course. (Please note, <u>three</u> is the maximum number, but you can select one or two if that accurately reflects your choice.)

This question has the effect of letting the respondent know that you are acknowledging there may be more than one reason influencing a choice. By restricting the choice to three, you prevent the respondent from selecting everything, which would make the question useless. By forcing a limit, the respondent will, you hope, identify the most important reasons.

Structuring the questionnaire

The overall look of a questionnaire, and the ordering of the questions, are very important. You need to maintain respondent motivation, especially with a long questionnaire. Make it easy for a respondent to want to take part, by using progressively graded questions that lead the respondent through the process. The questionnaire structure will greatly affect its reliability and validity.

Funnel and inverted funnel ordering

Always keep in mind that the person reading and responding to your questions is interpreting them in their own terms. The order of questions can send out unintentional messages about perceived intentions. In particular, the response to particular questions can be affected by the nature of the preceding ones. The funnel and inverted funnel techniques help to overcome this problem.

Funnel

The questionnaire begins with broadly-based questions and gradually works towards questions that have a narrow area of focus. The funnel technique is used:

1. where respondents are generally well-motivated

2. where the purpose of the survey is to obtain detailed information (the funnel approach helps respondents recall detailed information more efficiently)

3. where a particular question may impose a frame of reference before gaining respondents' views and so unduly influence the responses.

Here is an example of a simple funnel sequence of questions. Please note that they are not written in a questionnaire-friendly way; they simply illustrate the approach:

---

1. List some of the most important problems facing the European Union.
2. Which one of these problems do you think is the most important?
3. Why do you believe it is the most important?
4. Where do you find most of your information about this problem?
5. Which newspaper(s) do you read?

The overt agenda of this sequence is to see how opinion is related, if at all, to the sources of information and, more particularly, the newspapers read by respondents. The funnel sequence helps the respondent to focus on thinking about the problems, as a sort of warm up to asking the target question of what they believe is the most important issue, and how they are informed about this issue.

Notice that the newspaper question comes last. If it came earlier, it could bias the response to question 3 because the respondent may make all sorts of assumptions about the questionnaire's agenda.

Inverted funnel

As the name implies, the inverted funnel approach reverses the sequence. It starts with the narrower questions and develops into a broader view. This sequence is used:

1. where the subject matter is not likely to be very motivating, or is of little or no interest to respondents – a respondent is more likely to answer questions that are specific and easy, rather than generalised ones requiring more effort

2. where respondents' experiences of the subject matter is not very recent and memory may be hazy and unreliable (specific questions will help a respondent recall facts etc)

3. where the respondent will be asked to make an overall judgement about facts (i.e. narrow questions can establish facts first of all).

Here is an example of inverted funnel sequencing. Again, the questions are not meant to be taken as perfect examples, but simply to illustrate the process.

1. Which of the following issues did you discuss with your adviser?

2. After your discussions, which of the following actions were you able to take?

3. Did these actions in general have the desired outcome for you?

4. How would you rate the quality of the service you received from your adviser?

In this example, the target question is a general rating of service quality. However, as this type of question is often asked after the events concerned, it is often necessary to make the respondent recall the specifics of the event first so that a considered judgement is more likely to be made.

Filter questions

Some questions or sections of your questionnaire may apply to some respondents but not to others. If so, you may need to divert respondents away from inappropriate questions towards other parts of your questionnaire. You use a filter question that identifies which respondents need to answer which questions. The following is an example:

1. Do you live alone? If NO go straight to question 2. If YES go straight to question 4.

2. How many other people live in your household?

3. List the number of people in each of the following age groups . . .

4. On average, how often do you visit your local public library?

Question 1 is the filter question that directs respondents. If you fail to use this approach, respondents will become fed up with being exposed to questions that are irrelevant to them. They are more likely to not respond at all to the questionnaire. Again, it is a matter of making it easy for your respondents to do your bidding.

Pitfalls in questionnaire design

There are many pitfalls and potential gaffs to be made in designing your questionnaire. Some will make your respondents smile, but most will make your questionnaire look unprofessional.

Language and wording

Keep the wording of questions as straightforward as possible. Lengthy questions may lead to confusion and misunderstanding, as the reader needs to work at understanding them. Of course, there are occasions when an explanation is required, but these should be used sparingly and preferably where a number of responses will follow, such as scales, ratings, and multi-response items. In this way, the length of the question's preamble is in proportion to the amount of information gained.

The language and vocabulary should match the intended reader. The use of jargon is best avoided unless essential, or appropriate, to the intended readership. If technical terms need to be used with a lay readership, you will need to explain them.

The following is an example of two hypothetical questions in a health survey. The first is intended for medical practitioners. The second is for their patients:

1. How many of your patients were born with an ASD, VSD or AVSD?

2. To your knowledge, are you aware of any members of your family who were born with a 'hole in the heart' condition?

Leading or threatening questions

You are more likely to fall into the trap of asking leading questions rather than threatening ones. However, it can be quite surprising what your respondents may regard as threatening, using a broad definition of that word.

Leading questions

A leading question is one that gives the respondent the impression that you are looking for a particular response, or it gives a clear message about what are good or bad responses. Here is an example:

Would you say that you spend too much on clothes?

Apart from the problem of determining what 'too much' is, the question implies that you *can* spend too much, and that this may be undesirable. Some people who feel guilty about their spending, however large or small, might say YES. Others who regard themselves as moderate spenders will probably say NO. A better question might be:

On average, how much do you estimate you spend on clothes each month?

There are no socially value-laden messages in this question. It also allows you to quantify spending patterns, albeit as an estimate.

Threatening questions
These do not necessarily refer to a physical threat, but more to questioning of a respondent's values, beliefs and behaviour. Any question which implies that the respondent is not acting in a socially acceptable way is unlikely to be well received! Embarrassing questions are also potentially threatening. They may be seen as exposing the respondent to ridicule, or to an invasion of privacy.

In short, any question likely to arouse anxiety in respondents should be regarded as threatening. Responses to such questions are likely to be biased in a way that neutralises the threat.

Two questions in one
The respondent does not know how to respond because two or more responses are possible. Here is an example of 'two questions in one':

Drug abuse and violent crime are the most serious problems facing society today.

strongly agree	agree	not sure	disagree	strongly disagree

A respondent may agree that drug abuse is the most serious problem facing society, but that violent crime is less so. How does the respondent answer this question? It requires a scale of agreement that is common to both issues, but the respondent may not have equality of agreement.

Ordering the questions
The use of funnel and inverted funnel sequencing of questions addresses one area of questionnaire structure. However, a questionnaire may be complex and cover a number of areas. In this case you need to consider the overall sequence of questions carefully. The general rules are:

1. Ask the easy-to-answer questions first.

2.   Closed response questions are often better placed before open response questions as they generally require less work to answer.

3.   Questions that are complex, or relate to sensitive issues, should appear later in the questionnaire. This allows respondents to become comfortable with taking part, before being 'hit' with areas of difficulty. Also, a respondent will at least answer the early parts of the questionnaire before refusing to continue. You may still gain some useful data. A refusal to answer an early question is more likely to lead to refusal to complete the questionnaire.

The covering letter

The questionnaire may be part of a postal survey, as opposed to a survey carried out by an interviewer. If so, it must go with a covering letter that explains its purpose and how the information will be used. Most potential respondents couldn't care less about your question-naire, unless they have a vested interest in the subject. Where possible, establish the potential value of the survey to the reader. For example, you can say that the data will be used to improve services used by the reader.

A good covering letter should:

1.   identify the person or organisation carrying out the survey

2.   explain the purpose of the survey

3.   clearly explain why it is important for the reader to respond to the survey (i.e. address the reader's vested interest)

4.   address the issue of confidentiality. The reader must be confident that there is no potential to harm or embarrass. Of course, the requirements of the data protection act need to be observed. Will it be possible to identify an individual from any data published or passed on to a third party? These are important issues.

Finally, it is best practice to provide pre-paid return envelopes. Don't expect respondents to pay to send the completed questionaires back.

Piloting the questionnaire

A new questionnaire must be piloted (tested). It should be sent to a small sample of people, and their responses assessed to check the suitability of each question as well as the overall reception. You can now make modifications to remove problems in understanding questions, to reduce ambiguity, to identify new categories of response, and to generally tidy it up.

The pilot should be conducted under the same conditions as the real survey. Participants should be chosen using the same random process as the real survey. It is hard to be specific about the sample size for a pilot because it depends on the overall size of the survey, and the money and time available. Participants in the pilot should be excluded from the real survey.

Tutorial: helping you learn

Progress questions

1. What is meant by the terms (a) reliability and (b) validity, in relation to data collection and analysis?

2. What is meant by (a) open and closed response questions, and (b) single and multiple response questions, in relation to question structure?

3. What is meant by (a) funnel, and (b) inverted funnel, in regard to the ordering of questions?

4. Under what circumstances would you use a filter question?

5. What is the purpose of a covering letter in a postal survey?

Discussion points

1. In general, response rates from postal surveys are low. Potential respondents are unlikely to be motivated enough to invest time, or are suspicious of questionnaires. Around 25% is quite typical, although it can be much lower! A second mailing to non-respondents sometimes works, but rarely raises the response rate above 50%. Discuss other possible ways of motivating people to respond.

2.　After taking the trouble to design a postal survey – including carefully operationalised concepts and constructed questionnaire, and probability sampling of the target population to create a representative sample – you end up with a 25% response rate. Discuss the effect this response rate may have on the reliability and validity of your results.

Assignment

Design a questionnaire with covering letter on a subject or concept you are currently working on. Pilot the questionnaire with, say, 30 people. Don't forget to use probability sampling to select your sample. Assess the responses you receive, identifying the strengths and weaknesses of your questionnaire. Modify the questionnaire, if necessary, in the light of your assessment.

Study tips

Motivating people to respond to a questionnaire can be a major headache. You should always put yourself in the shoes of a potential respondent and honestly answer this question: 'If I were a member of the public receiving this questionnaire, would I respond?' Try to look at questionnaires produced by other people and organisations and identify the good and bad points. Make careful notes of good practice to use and bad practice to avoid.

7

Summarising Your Data: Frequency Tables and Charts

One-minute Overview – The first stage in examining your data set is to print a **frequency table** for each variable. This lists the number of responses for each item in a question, and allows you to examine the distribution of the data and identify possible **outliers** (values significantly higher than the rest). It can also help you identify **rogue values** values that are obviously mistakes. It is also useful to display the data in the form of charts or graphs that provide a more effective visual means of examining data distribution. The three commonly used charts are: **histograms, stem-and-leaf** charts, and **boxplots**. The first two help you form an impression of how well the data approximates **normal distribution**. Boxplots are very useful, not only for illustrating data distribution, but also for indicating the **central tendency** through the **median** (both these terms are discussed in more detail in the next chapter). In this chapter we will explore:

▶ univariate analysis
▶ frequency tables
▶ displaying data with charts and tables

Univariate analysis

When you have collected your data and entered it into a database or statistics software package, you will want to begin the process of analysis. The first stage is to look at each variable individually. This is called univariate analysis. There is little in the way of detailed analysis you can do when looking at the data for a single variable, but univariate analysis is useful for the following.

1. You can identify rogue values and outliers. See **Cleaning up the data set** later in this chapter.

2. You can look at the general distribution of the data to assess its spread. Is it all bunched up across a narrow range of values, or is it widely dispersed? Does the pattern of distribution of **interval data** approximate **normal distribution**? (Remember, some statistical techniques require the data to approximate a normal distribution pattern).

3. You can calculate some simple statistical **descriptives** that enable you to make some comparisons. These include **mean**, **median**, **standard deviation** and **interquartile** range, all of which are explained in chapter 8. Look on this chapter and chapter 8 as complementary.

Frequency tables

The first task after completing the data entry stage of your project is to generate a list of responses to each variable in the database. Frequency tables are generated. These will list the number of responses to each option (item) within a question.

Generating a frequency table

All spreadsheet and statistics software packages generate frequency tables. The tables and charts in this and later chapters have been generated using Excel or SPSS. (For a description of these packages see chapter 3.) Table 7.1 shows a frequency table generated by SPSS. The data for this table is found on the website (page for chapter 3) and is derived from the question about respondent age. There are several features that need to be explained.

Missing values

Not all your respondents will be willing to provide all the information you ask for. Age can be a sensitive question and may be left out. This then becomes a **missing value**. SPSS automatically identifies missing values and lists them separately, as you can see (3 cases). It will regard these cases as invalid and exclude them from any analysis requiring this information.

At other times you may want to exclude cases that have a particular value, and tell SPSS to classify this as a missing value.

Q1 Age

	Age	Frequency	Percent	Valid percent	Cumulative percent
Valid	21	4	1.6	1.6	1.6
	22	10	4.1	4.1	5.8
	23	12	4.9	4.9	10.7
	24	6	2.4	2.5	13.2
	25	11	4.5	4.5	17.7
	26	5	2.0	2.1	19.8
	27	11	4.5	4.5	24.3
	28	10	4.1	4.1	28.4
	29	4	1.6	1.6	30.0
	30	10	4.1	4.1	34.2
	31	12	4.9	4.9	39.1
	32	7	2.8	2.9	42.0
	33	6	2.4	2.5	44.4
	34	12	4.9	4.9	49.4
	35	12	4.9	4.9	54.3
	36	14	5.7	5.8	60.1
	37	14	5.7	5.8	65.8
	38	7	2.8	2.9	68.7
	39	9	3.7	3.7	72.4
	40	6	2.4	2.5	74.9
	41	7	2.8	2.9	77.8
	42	8	3.3	3.3	81.1
	43	6	2.4	2.5	83.5
	44	6	2.4	2.5	86.0
	45	6	2.4	2.5	88.5
	46	3	1.2	1.2	89.7
	47	7	2.8	2.9	92.6
	48	6	2.4	2.5	95.1
	49	4	1.6	1.6	96.7
	50	2	0.8	0.8	97.5
	51	1	0.4	0.4	97.9
	52	1	0.4	0.4	98.4
	53	1	0.4	0.4	98.8
	57	2	0.8	0.8	99.6
	64	1	0.4	0.4	100.0
	Total	243	98.8	100.0	
Missing	System	3	1.2		
Total		246	100.0		

Table 7.1. A frequency table generated by SPSS.

▶ *Example* – You may wish to exclude from a particular analysis everyone over 50 years of age. You will instruct SPSS to regard any age over 50 to be a missing value. If you now create a frequency table from the data, there will now be 9 missing values and only 237 valid cases in any subsequent analysis.

Statistics packages have this valuable facility. If you are using a spreadsheet package, you will probably have to remove these cases manually from the file, saving it as a file with a new name (to preserve the integrity of the original). This is very cumbersome, to say the least, and can lead to confusion. It is better to use a dedicated statistics package.

Cumulative percentage (cumulative frequency)

The first three column headings are straightforward:

1. *frequency* – is the number of cases of a given category of response

2. *percentage* – represents the frequency as a percentage of the total number of respondents

3. *valid percentage* – represents the frequency as a percentage of valid cases (i.e. it excludes the missing values).

Cumulative percentage adds up the valid percentage as it goes along. In other words, it adds the previous total percentage of valid cases to the current percentage.

▶ *Example* – 21-year-olds formed 1.6% of valid cases, and 22-year olds formed 4.1%. Therefore, 5.8% of cases are 22 years of age or less. So, by the same process, 28.4% of cases are 28-years old or less; 77.8% of cases are 41-years old or less; and 100% of cases are 64-years old or less.

Cumulative percentage is a useful measure for a number of reasons. For example, census returns to the Office for National Statistics are used to determine the age structure of the UK population. From these, insurance companies can construct **life tables** that show the cumulative frequency of age within the population (often separately for male and female, and even by geographical location). On the basis of these tables insurance premiums can be worked out, using the probability of surviving to or beyond a particular age.

Creating grouped frequency tables

The problem with table 7.1 is that it has so many categories, most of them with low numbers, that it is hard to see any pattern. It is too diffuse. With some variables, the number of categories is often small so that this is not a problem. **Interval** variables often present this difficulty. One way around this is to group the data into a smaller number of categories.

▶ *Example* – You might group together the ages into categories of 5 years as shown in table 7.2. This table was produced using SPSS. Note that the end value of each group is the same as the first value in the next group up. This is because age is a continuum in that you are 25 on the day before your 26th birthday. In other words by stating groups in this way, it is understood that the first group goes from 21 to 25 years and 364 days! More of this in chapter 8.

	Age group	Frequency	Percent	Valid percent	Cumulative percent
Valid	21 – 25	43	17.5	17.7	17.7
	26 – 30	40	16.3	16.5	34.2
	31 – 35	49	19.9	20.2	54.3
	36 – 40	50	20.3	20.6	74.9
	41 – 45	33	13.4	13.6	88.5
	46 – 50	22	8.9	9.1	97.5
	51 – 55	3	1.2	1.2	98.8
	56 – 60	2	0.8	0.8	99.6
	61 – 66	1	0.4	0.4	100.0
	Total	243	98.8	100.0	
Missing	System	3	1.2		
Total		246	100.0		

Table 7.2. A grouped frequency table.

The pattern of distribution is much clearer in table 7.2. There is a trade-off. On the one hand you will gain a clearer picture of the distribution of the data, but in the process you will lose the detail. Where possible, in any analysis of **interval** data, it is best to use ungrouped data. However, for presenting data to your readers, grouping it like this can make it easier to understand and to see patterns.

What is the best way to collapse the data into groups? There are no hard and fast rules. Be clear about what it is you are seeking to show with the data. Bear in mind that the greater the range within the group, the less detail can be seen. For example, if the groups had been based on ten years rather than five, there would have been far fewer categories, and the nature of the data distribution would have been masked.

Another point to remember is that interval data is not always a continuum. For example, marks in a test might be allocated as whole numbers, so the groupings may look more like this:

$$0-4, 5-9, 10-14, 15-19, \ldots \ldots$$

The distinction between data that is a continuum, and that clearly based on integers, is an important one when deciding on the group categories. Chapter 8 returns to the subject of grouped data.

The rest of this chapter is devoted to presenting data in a visual way. We can use special charting techniques to enable the viewer to identify patterns in the data distribution.

Displaying data with charts and graphs

Histograms

The best known form of chart described in this chapter is the histogram. Data is presented as a series of vertical bars, the length of which correspond to the frequencies. The histogram represents grouped data. Figure 7.1 is a histogram produced by SPSS from the grouped data in table 7.2.

Technically speaking, the area of each bar actually represents the frequency of respondents as a proportion of the entire sample. The total area of all the bars therefore represents the sample as a whole. This is visually more effective than tables of data at showing patterns of distribution.

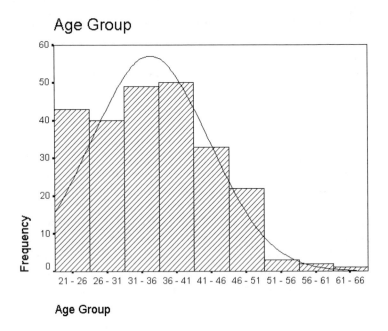

Figure 7.1. A histogram produced by SPSS from the grouped data in table 7.2

SPSS has a very useful facility: it allows you to put a normal distribution curve over the histogram so you can see if the distribution of your data approximates the normal distribution pattern. This distribution broadly approximates normal distribution, although it is a little flat to the left of the chart.

Stem-and-Leaf Chart

Most people will recognise a histogram, but a stem-and-leaf chart is less well known. Figure 7.2 shows a stem-and-leaf chart based on the data in table 7.1. Stem-and-leaf charts have the dual effect of representing the frequency of each category in a way that allows you to visually check the distribution, and also the number of cases within each category of the variable concerned.

The stem column usually represents the first digit of the category. At the bottom of the chart you are told that the stem width is 10. A stem of 2 really means 20 in this example. You are also told that each

```
Q1 Age Stem-and-Leaf Plot

 Frequency      Stem &  Leaf

      4.00         2 .  1111
     22.00         2 .  2222222222333333333333
     17.00         2 .  44444455555555555
     16.00         2 .  6666677777777777
     14.00         2 .  88888888889999
     22.00         3 .  0000000000111111111111
     13.00         3 .  2222222333333
     24.00         3 .  444444444444555555555555
     28.00         3 .  6666666666666667777777777777
     16.00         3 .  8888888999999999
     13.00         4 .  0000001111111
     14.00         4 .  22222222333333
     12.00         4 .  444444555555
     10.00         4 .  6667777777
     10.00         4 .  8888889999
      3.00         5 .  001
      2.00         5 .  23
       .00         5 .
      2.00         5 .  77
      1.00 Extremes    (>=64)

 Stem width:    10
 Each leaf:       1 case(s)
```

Figure 7.2. A stem-and-leaf chart based on the data in table 7.1

leaf represents one case. This helps you interpret the chart. So, taking the first row where there is a frequency of 4, these are all 21 year olds. In the second row, of the 22 listed, 10 cases are 22 years old and 12 are 23 years old, and so on. The stem width is made as large as is compatible with the data. For example, if the chart was representing data on people's height, a height of 173cm might be represented as:

$$\text{stem} \quad \text{leaf}$$
$$17 \quad 3$$
$$\text{stem width} \ = \ 10$$
$$\text{leaf} \ = \ 1 \text{ case}$$

Figure 7.2 was generated by SPSS, which has also identified 'extreme values', or **outliers**. This is dealt with later in the chapter, and you'll find more in chapter 8.

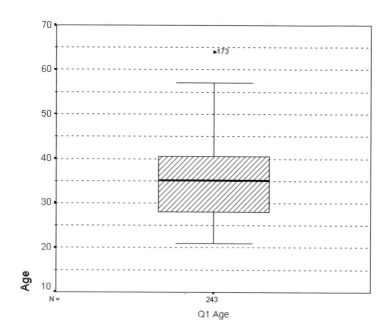

Figure 7.3. A boxplot of the data listed in table 7.1
(generated by SPSS).

Boxplots

These look at the distribution of data slightly differently. They chart the distribution on the basis of certain key measurements – essentially **central tendency**, discussed in the next chapter. These measurements are the **median**, **interquartile range**, and the **minimum** and **maximum** values. Chapter 8 explains them in detail. Figure 7.3 is a boxplot of the data listed in table 7.1 and was generated by SPSS.

The shaded rectangular area is the box and the two vertical lines that extend upwards like a 'T' and downwards like an inverted 'T' are called **whiskers**. The bold horizontal line cutting across the box marks the position of the median value (35 years). The upper and lower edges of the box represent the third and first quartiles (41 and 28 years) respectively. The box therefore represents the interquartile range. (See chapter 8).

The whiskers extend out to what the software has calculated to be the maximum and minimum values (57 and 21 years respectively).

Note: these values are not necessarily the same as the actual values. There is one respondent aged 64. As with the stem-and-leaf plot, it has been identified as an outlier or extreme value. A boxplot will plot outliers individually and the number beside the position is the record number in the database. In effect, a boxplot warns you about using these cases for any meaningful calculations.

Along the horizontal axis you will see a number (243). This is the number of cases included in the boxplot. The three cases whose ages are not known have been left out of the analysis by the software.

Cleaning up the data set

Frequency tables, boxplots, and stem-and-leaf charts – when generated by statistics software – provide you with valuable information about your data. This is particularly so regarding values that appear unreal, or that are at the extreme limits of the data.

▶ *Example 1* – If one of the cells in your database gave the age of a respondent as 993, all of these methods of summarising data would have picked it up. Common sense will tell you that this is a data entry mistake.

▶ *Example 2* – This could be in a question that requires a 'yes' or 'no'. If the coding options are 0 = No, 1 = Yes, 9 = No response, but you find a code of 3 in the tables or charts, you would regard this as an error. Such errors are called **rogue values** as would be an age of 993!

However, there will be times when the data is somewhat removed from the main bulk of the data values, but you cannot reasonably say that it is an error. In table 7.1, one mature undergraduate has given her age as 64. Of course, there could be a 64 year-old undergraduate (there are actually quite a number in higher education), so you cannot call it an error. A value that is reasonable, but which lies far removed from the main data, is called an **outlier** or **extreme value**.

Using SPSS and Excel

MicroSoft Excel is an excellent tool for producing high quality graphs and charts. Use the 'chart wizard' facility to lead you through the process of generating a graph. However, Excel does not produce boxplots or stem-and-leaf charts.

For these charts, SPSS is the better tool. Until now, the quality of the graphical output from SPSS has been arguably less impressive than that of Excel, but version 8 of SPSS is excellent. It rivals Excel in many ways, particularly for the level of detail you can add to each graph and chart. Stem-and-leaf and boxplots are effective in helping you identify outliers. Use the 'graphs' command on the menu bar to generate your chart.

Dealing with rogue values and outliers

Rogue values

Rogue values should be corrected whenever possible. You will need to go back to the original questionnaire – if you can identify it – and check the appropriate response. The database record can then corrected. If this cannot be done, for whatever reason, it is vital not to guess what the response 'should' have been. This is widely regarded as unethical (faking!). It also introduces bias into the process. It is *your* response rather than that of the respondent. It would be better to treat the response as a **missing value**.

Outliers

Outliers can present something of a dilemma. They are discussed further in chapter 8. It is sometimes best to regard outliers as missing values, because of their potential to distort the findings of your survey. For example, if you are looking at the relationship between employment and participation in higher education, you may want to exclude the 64 year-old woman. On the other hand, if you are looking at general motivational factors, you may want to include her.

As you will see in chapter 8, outliers can have a significant effect on the calculation of some key descriptive statistics. In such cases, exclude them from your analysis, but give reasons, justifying them on methodological grounds.

Tutorial: helping you learn

Progress questions

1. What are meant by the terms: frequency, missing values, grouped data, cumulative frequency?

2. What is meant by the terms: outlier, and rogue value?

3. What are the advantages of displaying data in each of the following forms: histogram, stem-and-leaf chart, boxplot?

Discussion points

1. In a frequency table where the variable values range from 1 to 100, it is cumbersome to try and present the frequency of each value in a report. You need to group the data. Suggest possible groupings, justifying your choices, if the variables were (a) annual number of visits to the cinema, (b) weekly shopping bill in pounds sterling, and (c) number of cars coming off the production line every day. Clue: this discussion will revolve around whether or not a variable is a continuum as this will determine cut-off and starting points for each data group.

2. You have to produce a short report comparing the salaries of staff in different organisations and to present the data in graphical format. Explain your choice of graphical representation, and include an explanation of why you had rejected other forms of graphical representation.

Assignment

The assignment in chapter 1 asked you to carry out a survey of traffic flow past a landmark over the same period on two consecutive days. Take this data and write a short report comparing traffic flow differences (a) between two consecutive days, and (b) between categories of vehicles. Make sure you include appropriate frequency tables and charts.

Study tips

1. It is usual to provide at least one basic statistical measure as well as a visual presentation of the data. Typical measures are described in chapter 8. You may prefer to read the next chapter before tackling the assignment or discussion points.

2. Only use frequency tables and charts to summarise your findings if you have a worthwhile point to make. A table or chart without an explanation (better still, an analysis) makes the exercise pointless. Examine some official reports and journals to see how their authors have done this. Also, look at statistical digests produced by the Office for National Statistics (ONS) such as *Social Trends*, *Annual Abstract of Statistics*, and *Regional Trends*. These carry summary reports as well as masses of statistical tables.

8

Summarising Your Data:
Central Tendency and Dispersion

One-minute Overview – It is often useful, and necessary, to summarise data in a way that allows the flavour of the data to be examined. One approach is to use 'measures of central tendency and dispersion'. The main measures of central tendency are the **mean** and **median**. The mode is also occasionally used but is of little value. The main measures of dispersion are **standard deviation** (based on the mean) and the **interquartile range** (based on the median). If the mean and the median are very similar, the distribution of data is likely to be symmetrical – or nearly so – and approximate the normal distribution. If there is a large difference between them, the distribution will be **skewed**. The measures described in this chapter require the data to be of **interval** type. In the case of standard deviation, it should approximate a normal distribution. In this chapter we will explore:

▶ number type
▶ measures of central tendency
▶ measures of dispersion
▶ standard error of measurement (SE)
▶ using SPSS and Excel

Number type

In this chapter the emphasis is on the calculation of summary data. You can apply the techniques in this chapter only to **interval** numbers.

Measures of central tendency

One way of summarising data is to determine a value that is typical of the sample as a whole. There are three main measures that are used.

The first two, the **mean** and **median** values, are important for a number of reasons. One is to tell us whether the data approximates the **normal distribution pattern**. The third measure, the **mode** is little used, although it can sometimes be helpful.

Mean

To most people 'mean' means 'average'. To use its correct title, it is called arithmetical mean, and it is calculated like this:

$$\text{mean} = \frac{\text{sum (total) of the values}}{\text{number of cases}}$$

Weighted mean

Almost always, you will be dealing with data in which the frequency of a given value will be more than one. Consider the frequency table (table 8.1), which summarises the ages of a sample of mature students. It is one of the frequency tables used in chapter 7.

Mean of grouped data

Sometimes there are a large number of categories, some of them with very low frequencies. They need to be 'collapsed' into a smaller number of categories by creating groups of equal intervals.

It is possible to calculate the mean value from those groups. We assume the typical value is the mid-point, and multiply this by the group frequency to arrive at the weighted mean. Table 8.2 shows how to do this using the data in table 8.1 based on the response to the question: 'What was your age at your last birthday?'

Age group	Limits	Mid-point	Frequency	Midpoint x Frequency
21 – 26	21 – 25.9	23.5	43	1010.5
26 – 31	26 – 30.9	28.5	40	1140
31 – 36	31 – 35.9	33.5	49	1641.5
36 – 41	36 – 40.9	38.5	50	1925
41 – 46	41 – 45.9	43.5	33	1435.5
46 – 51	46 – 50.9	48.5	22	1067
51 – 56	51 – 55.9	53.5	3	160.5
56 – 61	56 – 60.9	58.5	2	117
61 – 66	61 – 65.9	63.5	1	63.5
TOTALS			**243**	**8560.5**
Arithmetic Mean = 8560.5/243 =				**35.2**

Table 8.2. Calculating the mean value from groups.

Age	Frequency	Frequency X Age
21	4	84
22	10	220
23	12	276
24	6	144
25	11	265
26	5	130
27	11	297
28	10	280
29	4	116
30	10	300
31	12	372
32	7	224
33	6	198
34	12	408
35	12	420
36	14	504
37	14	518
38	7	266
39	9	351
40	6	240
41	7	287
42	8	336
43	6	258
44	6	264
45	6	270
46	3	138
47	7	329
48	6	288
49	4	196
50	2	100
51	1	51
52	1	52
53	1	53
57	1	114
64	1	64
TOTALS	243	8423

Mean Age = 8423/243 = 34.7

Table 8.1. A frequency table summarising the ages of a sample of mature students.

There is a small error introduced into the sum of **mid-point X frequency** (8560.5 as opposed to 8423). The arithmetical mean is 35.2 years. The **limits** column shows the minimum and maximum value of the group.

The final result will be a close approximation. You just need to be aware that there may be a relatively small error in the result. One way of overcoming that is to use groupings in which the interval between minimum and maximum group value is quite small. For example, an interval of 5 (such as '21–26') is likely to produce a smaller error than an interval of 10 (such as '21–31').

A problem with the mean

The mean is susceptible to distortion by extreme values. The mean is supposed to give us a representative value of a range of values. A simple illustration shows how this can be upset:

Example A	2, 5, 6, 8, 11, 13	mean = 7.5
Example B	2, 5, 6, 8, 11, 55	mean = 14.5

Example B contains an extreme value (55) that is distorting, or skewing, the mean, making it unrepresentative of the sample. A mean of 7.5 is representative of example A, but in example B, a mean of 14.5 is skewed towards the extreme end, which does not make it truly representative.

Imagine that the numbers in both lists represented salaries in £10,000s in two small companies (where the owner-manager had the highest salary). Both companies may want to portray themselves as offering very good salaries. Company B looks very attractive with an average salary of £140,500, as opposed to £75,000 at company A.

There are two ways around this problem:

1. Identify the extreme values and exclude them from the calculations. There is no problem about doing this, so long as you are honest. Just explain to the reader that your calculations have been based on adjusted figures.

2. Use a different measure for central tendency that is much less susceptible to this kind of distortion.

Median

The median is the measure of central tendency less likely to be subject to distortion by extreme values. The median is the middle value in a range of values. Again, this can best be illustrated by a simple example:

Example A	2, 5, 6, 8, 11, 13	median = 7
Example B	2, 5, 6, 8, 11, 55	median = 7

Where there is an odd number of cases, the median will always be the number in the middle. For example, if there are seven cases, the median is the value of the fourth case. Where there is an even number of cases, as above, the median value lies between 6 and 8 – in other words 7, effectively the mean of 6 and 8.

There is another way of looking at the median. It is the value where there are exactly 50% of cases below and above this value. That makes it important because it is fixed; you know where it is placed in your sample. The mean is not fixed like this.

It is often useful to calculate the mean and the median values for a variable and then compare them. A large difference between them should warn us that the values are somehow skewed by the presence of extreme values. In the examples used above, both values are very close – the mean is 34.7 and the median is 35.

Mean, median and skew

The mean and median of any set of data tell you something quite important about its distribution. In the perfect example of **normal distribution**, the mean and median values will be identical because 50% of cases will be below the mean and 50% will be above it. This is the definition of the median!

Where the distribution is not symmetrical about the mean, it is **skewed**. Figure 8.1 revisits skew. Where the mean is significantly higher than the median, this is positive skew. Where the mean is significantly lower than the median, it is negative skew.

In practice, very few data sets will show a perfect normal distribution, but if the skew is pronounced (i.e. the difference between the mean and median quite large), then the data must be treated with caution if a technique assumes normal distribution.

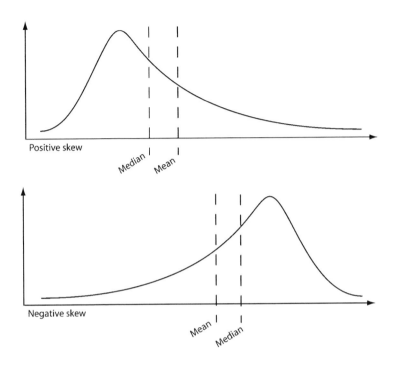

Figure 8.1. Positive and negative skew.

Mode

The mode is of little value in statistics. It is the most *commonly occurring* value within the data. In table 8.1, there are two modal values, 36 and 37 years of age. The mode tells you where the peak of the distribution lies. Where mode does become interesting is if you detect two or more modal values that are not adjacent to each other, creating two peaks. This might just be the result of your sample containing two different groups of individuals, each with its own mean and median. It would be worth exploring this with tests of significance, such as a 'comparison of means' which we will cover later in the book.

Measures of dispersion

Another useful piece of information about your data is how far it is
spread out. The mean and median tell you where the middle values
tend to lie, but nothing about the *spread* of data. Statisticians want to
know how data is dispersed, and there are several ways of measuring
this.

Range, minimum and maximum values

The minimum and maximum values of any data set are self-
explanatory – they are simply the lowest and highest values
respectively. The **range** is simply the difference between these two
values.

▶ *Example* – In table 8.1, the minimum and maximum values of
mature student ages are 21 and 64. This gives a range of 43 years.

It is not enough to know the mean value. The mean for that data
set is 34.7 years, but if you did not have access to the raw data you
would not know how widely dispersed the ages are. For example, it
would still be possible to have a mean of 34.7 years, while the youngest
could be 30 and the oldest 39!

Scales and ranges in questionnaires

There are many circumstances when knowing the range is important.
Suppose you are developing a scale for use in a questionnaire (see
chapter 5). You will want to see a large range in the distribution of
data for any single item in the scale. This makes the item very good at
discriminating between individuals, because it is a more sensitive
measure. If the data is all bunched together, it is not a good measure
as it has poor discriminatory power.

Psychological tests

Another example of range is psychological tests. If you were to devise
a test to assess numerical ability, you would want to be able to
discriminate between individuals in a way that reflects our assumption of a wide range of ability levels across a population. If your test
was producing data very closely bunched together, it is probably not
reflecting this, and the test would not be a good one.

Standard deviation and variance

These two measures are closely related, mathematically speaking. Their value is to provide a standardised way of measuring dispersion. This allows comparisons to be made between one group of data and another. Table 8.1 shows the age distribution of mature students at college X. If you were to collect similar data for college Y and calculated the mean and median values, they might be very similar. However, the spread of ages could be very different.

Standard deviation

Table 8.3 illustrates the point by adding an extra statistic called the **standard deviation** that describes the spread of values about the mean:

	College X	College Y
mean	34.7	35.0
median	35.0	34.8
standard deviation	8.4	4.3

Table 8.3. Standard deviation, describing the spread of values about the mean.

The standard deviation tells you that college X has a wider spread of ages around the mean within its mature student population than college Y. College Y has a more homogeneous group of mature students with respect to age. This may also mean that there are some other important (statistically significant) differences between them.

Any statistical or spreadsheet software package such as SPSS and Excel – even the simplest of pocket 'scientific' calculators – calculate most statistics you need very easily. The need to learn formulae by heart tends to be a thing of the past.

The importance of standard deviation

Standard deviation requires your data distribution to at least approximate normal distribution. Figure 8.2 shows the distribution of ages for mature students using table 8.1 as the source table and it approximates a normal distribution. Five vertical lines have been

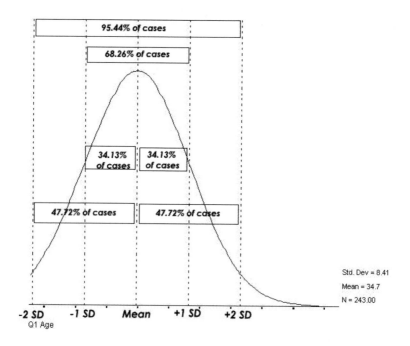

Figure 8.2. The age distribution of mature students.

drawn on the graph and are positioned at: the mean, at 1 and 2 standard deviations (SD) above the mean, and at 1 and 2 standard deviations below the mean. The lines mark the positions of the following ages:

$$
\begin{array}{ll}
34.7 & (\text{mean}) \\
26.3 & (\text{mean} - 1\text{SD}) \\
17.9 & (\text{mean} - 2\text{SD}) \\
43.1 & (\text{mean} + 1\text{SD}) \\
51.5 & (\text{mean} + 2\text{SD}).
\end{array}
$$

Of course, there was no-one aged less than 21 in the sample, so 17.9 is effectively off the scale in this example, but that does not alter the importance of what is being described here.

Standard deviation divides a normal distribution curve into distinct proportions. 68.26% of cases will lie within 1 standard deviation from the mean (i.e. approximately two thirds), 34.13%

above and 34.13% below. At two standard deviations above and below the mean, 95.44% of cases fall within that range (47.72% of cases each side of the mean). At three standard deviations, the estimated proportion of cases that would fall within that range is 99.7% (49.85% on each side). Table 8.4 summarises this for the data in table 8.1.

Number of standard deviations	% cases within the range	Range in table 1
1	68.26	26.3 and 43.1 years
2	95.44	17.8* and 51.5 years
3	99.7	9.5* and 59.9 years

Table 8.4. A summary of three standard deviations.
*Common sense is needed when interpreting this sort of data. Clearly there is no-one aged 9 or 17 in the sample, so some caution is always required when making statements about the significance of any results. Check out the numbers first.

Variance
You will tend to use standard deviation rather more than variance, since it has much more practical value. However, some statistical techniques do use variance, which is very closely related to it. Variance is a measure of the spread of the data. It can be calculated from the standard deviation very easily. Standard deviation is the square root of the variance. So, taking the example of student ages given above where the standard deviation is 7.2 years, the variance will be 51.8 (in other words, 7.2 x 7.2).

Z-scores
We can express a particular variable value in terms of the standard deviation of the variable. The Z-score represents a value as the number of standard deviations above or below the mean. You can then use this information to work out the proportion of cases that fall above or below that score, or between two scores. The assumption is that the scores are normally distributed. You calculate a value's Z-score like this:

Statistics for Social Sciences

$$Z = \frac{(\text{value} - \text{mean})}{\text{standard deviation}}$$

Suppose a student scores 38 marks on an examination paper. The mean score is 48 and the standard deviation is 7. This student's Z-score is:

$$Z = (38{-}48) \div 7 = -10/7 = -1.43$$

In other words, the student's score lies 1.43 standard deviations below the mean. By referring to a **table of Z-scores** in a book of statistical tables, the student can be placed on the normal distribution curve as shown in figure 8.3. 42% of scores will lie between 38 and the mean of 48. Put another way, 92% of students will have scored better!

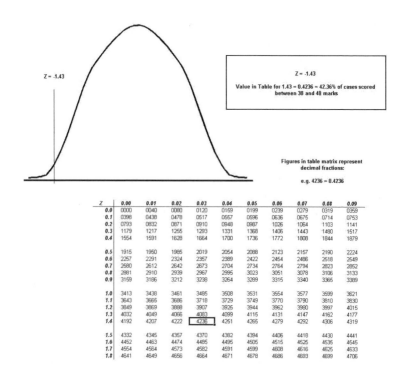

Z = -1.43

Value in Table for 1.43 = 0.4236 = 42.36% of cases scored between 38 and 48 marks

Figures in table matrix represent decimal fractions:

e.g. 4236 = 0.4236

Z	0.00	0.01	0.02	0.03	0.04	0.05	0.06	0.07	0.08	0.09
0.0	0000	0040	0080	0120	0159	0199	0239	0279	0319	0359
0.1	0398	0438	0478	0517	0557	0596	0636	0675	0714	0753
0.2	0793	0832	0871	0910	0948	0987	1026	1064	1103	1141
0.3	1179	1217	1255	1293	1331	1368	1406	1443	1480	1517
0.4	1554	1591	1628	1664	1700	1736	1772	1808	1844	1879
0.5	1915	1950	1985	2019	2054	2088	2123	2157	2190	2224
0.6	2257	2291	2324	2357	2389	2422	2454	2486	2518	2549
0.7	2580	2612	2642	2673	2704	2734	2764	2794	2823	2852
0.8	2881	2910	2939	2967	2995	3023	3051	3078	3106	3133
0.9	3159	3186	3212	3238	3264	3289	3315	3340	3365	3389
1.0	3413	3438	3461	3485	3508	3531	3554	3577	3599	3621
1.1	3643	3665	3686	3718	3729	3749	3770	3790	3810	3830
1.2	3849	3869	3888	3907	3925	3944	3962	3980	3997	4015
1.3	4032	4049	4066	4083	4099	4115	4131	4147	4162	4177
1.4	4192	4207	4222	4236	4251	4265	4279	4292	4306	4319
1.5	4332	4345	4357	4370	4382	4394	4406	4418	4430	4441
1.6	4452	4463	4474	4484	4495	4505	4515	4525	4535	4545
1.7	4554	4564	4573	4582	4591	4599	4608	4616	4625	4633
1.8	4641	4649	4656	4664	4671	4678	4686	4693	4699	4706

Figure 8.3. A normal distribution curve.

The Z-score is useful in psychology and educational research, because it allows the researcher to standardise results. For example, in aptitude tests a subject's score can be compared to that of a **norm group**, a large representative sample of subjects.

In education, children of a given age are tested using assessment papers that are different each year (in the UK these include GCSE, SATs, A levels). It is impossible to guarantee that the standard of the papers is exactly the same every year. Assuming that the distribution of ability amongst children remains the same each year, any variation in distribution of scores will be explained by differences in the degree of difficulty of the exam papers. By converting actual marks to Z-scores for that year, it is possible to allocate grades and passes and fails on the basis of these comparisons. Consequently, the threshold scores between grades can fluctuate slightly year to year.

Quartiles and interquartile range

Another measure used to describe the spread of data is based on the **median** value as the point of centrality rather than the mean. It uses three fixed points based on the numbers of cases below that particular point. The fixed points are called **quartiles**.

▶ *The first quartile* – the value that represents the point where 25% of cases lie below it.

▶ *The third quartile* – the value that represents the point where 75% of cases lie below it.

▶ *The second quartile* – is of course the median.

▶ *The interquartile range* – the difference in value between the first and third quartile.

This has the advantage of not being affected by extreme values. It is not directly reliant upon the values themselves, but on the number of cases. This makes it valuable in making direct comparisons between groups. Comparing the interquartile range and median salaries helps overcome the problem of extreme values described earlier.

Another common use of quartiles is in standardised tests used in psychology, such as aptitude or personality tests. These often use **percentiles** as a means of measuring performance. If a value is at the 10th percentile, this means that there are 10% of cases below this value (and 90% above it, of course). It is possible, therefore to divide up the data into groups like this. The usual variations are **deciles** (based on 10% groupings) and **percentiles** (based on 1% groupings).

Standard error of measurement (SE)

Remember, you will normally be working with a sample drawn from **a population,** rather than with the entire population. All the measures described in this and other chapters describe the sample, not the population as a whole. A sample may not be a perfect representation of the population, so there will be problems if you try to make generalised statements about the whole population.

The 'standard error of measurement' helps get around that problem.

▶ *The concept* – If you draw a random sample from your population and calculate a statistical measure, you will arrive at a set of values. If you now repeat the process of randomly drawing your sample from the whole population, the membership of the second sample would be different to the first. Of course, some of the original sample members may be there, but it would still be a different sample. After calculating your statistic again it may be different. For example, the mean age of the first sample may have been 32 and that of the second 34. If you were to repeat this process many times, you would expect to have a range of values for your mean age. If you plotted a histogram or stem and leaf chart, you would expect a normal distribution, with clustering around the mean of the means.

This 'mean of means' is likely to be the true mean of the population. However, it could be any of the other values! If you calculate the standard deviation of these values you can create **limits of confidence.** For example, if the mean of your sample measure is 30, and the standard deviation is 2, you can be '68% confident' that the real value lies between 28 and 32, and '95% confident' that it lies between 26 and 34. This special case of standard deviation is called the **standard error of measurement.** It recognises that all measurements are subject to error and is a way of quantifying the error.

Calculating standard error from your sample

The formula is:

$$\text{standard error} = \frac{\text{standard deviate of variable}}{\sqrt{\text{ sample size}}}$$

$$\sqrt{} = \text{square root}$$

Using SPSS and Excel

Both SPSS and Excel will calculate all the measures described in this chapter. There is no need to memorise formulae or to undertake detailed arithmetic.

▶ *Using SPSS* – Select *Statistics* > *Summarise* > *Frequencies* to create frequency tables and several of the summary statistics such as mean, median, mode, quartiles. Another approach is to use the *Statistics* > *Summarise* > *Explore* option. This will print out detailed summary statistics. You can even ask the program to identify extreme values for you.

▶ *Using Excel* – Excel also has an excellent statistical summary function. You will find this in the *Data Analysis* option in the *Tools* menu. This feature is an *Add-in* and may not be installed on your computer. However, you can use the *Add-in* command to install this toolkit. Select the *Descriptive Statistics* option in the *Data Analysis* list.

Tutorial: helping you learn

Progress questions

1. Explain the difference between (a) mean and median, and (b) standard deviation and interquartile range.

2. If the mean score in a survey of attitudes towards televised sport is 70, and the standard deviation is 20, what range of scores would fall within the (a) 68% confidence limit; (b) 95% confidence limits; (c) 99% confidence limits?

3. Why are the median and interquartile range not influenced by extreme values and outliers?

4. The mean age of a sample of people is 25. The standard error is 1.5. Using the 95% confidence limit, what range is the actual mean age of the population likely to be?

5. Calculate the standard error in the mean monthly consumption of chocolate bars in a population if the sample size is 900 and the standard deviation of the number of bars consumed each month is 3.

Discussion point

The survey described in progress question 2 was given to another sample of people. The mean was found to be 85 and the median was 60. Since the maximum score is 100, discuss the nature of the distribution of scores and what this tells you about the sample of people surveyed.

Assignment

Using the database you set up during the assignment for chapter 3, generate means, medians, standard deviations, and interquartile ranges for all the interval variables. Look at each of these measures and comment on the extent to which the distributions approximate normal distribution. Also, calculate the standard error of measurement for each of these and determine the 95% confidence limits for each.

Study tips

The techniques described in chapter 7 and this chapter should not be treated as two separate approaches to initial analysis of data. So, when you are creating frequency tables and charts of your data, you should also calculate the statistical measures described in this chapter for interval measures, or scales that can be treated as interval.

9

Hypothesis Testing

One-minute Overview – Analysing your data is based on testing a **research hypothesis.** Data analysis is a systematic approach to finding evidence to support an idea you may have about the relationship between two or more variables. You will need to demonstrate that the data is unlikely to have been gained by chance alone. In other words, the **null hypothesis** (there is no real relationship between the variables) can be rejected, and your research hypothesis accepted if the probability of the null hypothesis being correct is less than 0.05. The test used is called **statistical significance** and there are a number of common tests used. These fall into two main categories: **parametric** and **non-parametric** tests. The choice depends on the nature of the data itself. The common parametric tests are **T-test** and **F-test** (based on means and variance). The common non-parametric test is the **chi-square test**, based on a comparison of actual and expected results. There is still always the risk of error. If you reject the null hypothesis when it is in fact correct, you will be committing a **Type I error**. If you accept the null hypothesis when it is, in fact, incorrect, you will have committed a **Type II error**. In this chapter we will explore:

▶ hypothesis testing
▶ causal and associative relationships
▶ the null-hypothesis *v* the research hypothesis
▶ tests of statistical significance
▶ parametric tests
▶ non-parametric tests

Hypothesis testing

Chapter 4 described the **research hypothesis** and the **research questions** you need to identify so that data can be collected to test the hypothesis. After collecting the data, you need to interrogate it using your software application (such as SPSS or Excel) to look for relationships between variables that would support your hypothesis. This is called hypothesis testing.

Causal and associative relationships

There are several possible ways of interpreting, or explaining, an observed relationship between variables.

Spurious relationship

An observed relationship between two variables, 'A' and 'B', may actually be caused by a third variable, 'C', that has not been observed, or whose effect has not been recognised. There is, in fact, no causal relationship between the observed variables 'A' and 'B'. Figure 9.1 illustrates this idea. Perhaps the easiest way to explain what can sometimes be an embarrassing error is to use a ridiculous example.

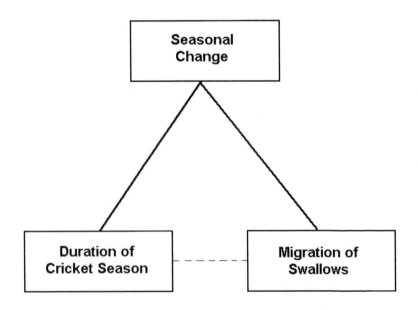

Figure 9.1. Two variables without a causal relationship.

▶ *Example* – There is an apparent association between the duration of the cricket season and the migratory behaviour of swallows. A fundamental error would be to assume that one caused the other! The true causal factor is the changing seasons.

The message is simple. Treat all observed relationships with caution at first until you have eliminated, as best you can, all other possible causal variables.

Intervening variables

There may be a causal relationship between two variables, but it is not necessarily a direct one. There may be an intervening variable. Figure 9.2 illustrates this.

One observed and frequently reported relationship is between gender and career progression. It is often noted that women do not generally progress as far as men in their careers. One stated reason for this observation is the role that women play within the family. Family commitments represent an 'intervening variable' that has a causal impact on career progression. While there is a direct association between gender and careers, this arises because of the intervening variable. Since it is women that usually take on that family role, the effect is more usually observed with them. It is probable that if a male took on the role described by the intervening variable (and more men have been doing so), you would find a similar effect on their career progression.

Interacting variables

In reality, it is often difficult to pinpoint one causal association. This is because human physical and psychological make-up, social circumstances and opportunities have profound effects on the way each individual views, interprets and reacts to the world. As a result, several or many variables often interact with each other and influence the observed relationship between two variables (chapter 10).

Figure 9.2. A causal relationship based on an intervening variable.

▶ *Example* – Looking back at figure 9.2, there are probably influences other than the fact that an individual has childcare responsibilities. The opportunity to work and bring up children at the same time, the attitudes of partners towards work and parental responsibilities, the financial status of the family group, and perhaps many other factors, will interact and influence the observed relationship.

An important function of social research and statistics is to identify the influences and to explain them. Statistics cannot explain, but they can go a long way towards identifying potential causal relationships.

The null-hypothesis v the research hypothesis

Suppose your research hypothesis is that: 'Job satisfaction increases as employees' salaries increase'. You will want to look for evidence in the research data. For example, if you have devised a job satisfaction index you would compare this with employee salaries to see if there is a direct relationship – is the job satisfaction index highest in respondents whose salaries are highest?

Statistical significance
The problem is that while you may *observe* a relationship, this is not *proof* that one exists. **Sampling error** may have resulted in your obtaining this finding through chance, because your data has been collected from a sample, not the entire population. To get around this problem, you have to return to probability theory to calculate the likelihood of your results being obtained by chance.

The test used is called **statistical significance**. This involves comparing the results of your research hypothesis with the results of the null hypothesis. The null hypothesis asserts that there is no relationship between the variables. The test of significance is to calculate the probability of obtaining your results by chance. If the probability of having gained your observations by chance were high, you would have to accept the null hypothesis. In other words, you would reject your research hypothesis.

Statisticians generally accept that you would only *tentatively* accept the research hypothesis, and reject the null hypothesis, if the probability of obtaining your results by chance alone was less that 5% ($p < 0.05$). In other words, you would be at least 95% confident that your research hypothesis is valid.

There are two other levels frequently used: 1% ($p < 0.01$, 99% confidence level) and 0.1% ($p < 0.001$, 99.9% confidence level) The lower the probability, the happier you should be with your hypothesis. The risk still remains that you can accept or reject your research hypothesis in error, but in good faith on the basis of statistical significance and you must always be cautious about your decisions.

In practice, the confidence level is chosen depending on the potential consequences of making a mistake. If accepting the research hypothesis would lead to radical changes in social policy affecting the lives of very many people, you would want to exercise caution and use $p < 0.01$ or even $p < 0.001$ as your threshold. You would want to reduce the risk of committing an error whose consequences could be very unfortunate.

Type I and Type II errors

Even after assessing statistical significance there is still the risk of accepting or rejecting the research hypothesis in error. Statisticians have identified two types of error:

1. A *Type I* (type one) error occurs if the *null hypothesis* is rejected when it is in fact correct. This is sometimes referred to as a false positive since the researcher has accepted a false *research hypothesis*.

2. A *Type II* (type two) error occurs if the *null hypothesis* is accepted when in fact the *research hypothesis* is correct. This is sometimes referred to as a *false negative* as the researcher has rejected a correct *research hypothesis*.

Table 9.1 summarises this principle.

		In reality	
		Null hypothesis correct	*Null hypothesis incorrect*
Resarch observations	*Null hypothesis rejected*	**Type I error**	Correct decision
	Null hypothesis accepted	Correct decision	**Type II error**

Table 9.1. Type I and Type II errors.

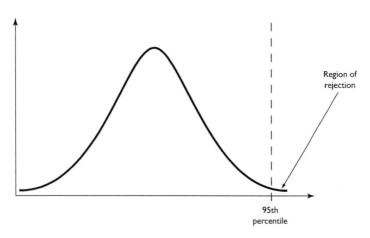

Figure 9.3. The normal distribution curve for all possible observations.

One- and two-tailed tests of significance

Figure 9.3, which is the normal distribution curve for all possible observations, shows the **region of rejection** looked for in a test of significance. If the likelihood of obtaining a result by chance alone is less than 5%, you will probably reject the null hypothesis. Your observations will be an extreme value within the range of possibilities.

This is fine so long as you know in which direction your research hypothesis predicts the observed results should be (i.e. it is a **directional hypothesis**). In the case of figure 9.3, the research hypothesis predicts that the result will be at the higher end of the distribution. Equally, your hypothesis might predict an outcome at the lower end of the distribution. For example, you may have a hypothesis that predicts absenteeism from work is lower in those employees who are highly motivated.

Where the research hypothesis is directional you would use what is termed a one-tailed test of significance. Figure 9.3 shows the region of rejection of the null hypothesis as lying within the area representing 5% ($p < 0.05$) of possible outcomes. Depending on the predicted direction, this could be the top 5% or the bottom 5%. It is called a one-tailed test because the region of rejection is limited to one tail of the distribution of possible outcomes.

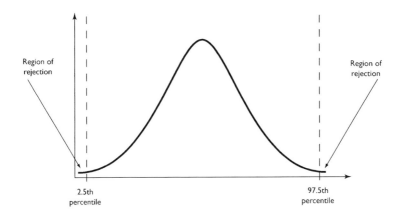

Figure 9.4. How the probability of obtaining observations by chance is distributed.

Most hypotheses are directional because that is the nature of prediction. However, there may be times when a hypothesis is non-directional. If this is the case – and you hypothesize a casual link between two variables, but cannot predict in which direction – then the two-tailed test of significance is invoked. Figure 9.4 shows how the probability of obtaining your observations by chance is now distributed.

Taking $p < 0.05$, you would now reject the null hypothesis if your observations fall within the top or bottom 2.5% of possible outcomes. In other words, since you are not predicting a direction to your outcome, your hypothesis is weaker. The 5% region of rejection has to be shared between both ends of the distribution of possible outcomes. This makes it harder to reject the null hypothesis, and you are in greater danger of committing a Type II error. It is better to test directional hypotheses and use one-tailed tests of significance.

Degrees of freedom

'Degrees of freedom' refers to the number of components in our results that are free to vary. It can be a difficult concept to master. However, a simple example will show the idea. Table 9.2 shows the results of a hypothetical survey into the colours of cars preferred by men.

Preferred colour	Frequency
black	25
blue	61
green	15
red	85
white	40
yellow	5
Total	231

Table 9.2. Table illustrating 'degrees of freedom'.

You want to know if this distribution of choices is statistically significant, and whether it shows that men are likely to be attracted to buying red cars in preference to other colours. To determine this you need to know the degrees of freedom and then apply your statistical test. The result of a test is a number that you need to look up against the degrees of freedom in tables designed for the test. There are five degrees of freedom in this example because if the value of one of the categories was known, the other five are free to vary so long as the total came to 231.

The 'rule of thumb' approach is to calculate the degrees of freedom as:

$$\text{degrees of freedom} = \text{number of categories} - 1$$

Both Excel and SPSS will undertake tests of statistical significance for you, and you will not need to use statistical tables.

Tests of statistical significance

Several common tests can be used to assess the statistical significance of your findings. The choice depends on the data you are working with. Many text books contain the formulae required for these tests, but computer software packages make the task quicker – and arguably freer of error – than working by hand. The main thing is to understand the principles and know how to apply the right test in any given set of circumstances.

There are two major groups of tests: parametric and non-parametric. Tests of significance do assume that you have used random sampling techniques to draw your research sample.

Parametric tests

These tests are applied when you can make two assumptions about your data:

1. The samples have been drawn from a population in which the variables concerned are normally distributed.

2. The variables are on an **interval** scale.

Non-parametric tests

These tests make much weaker assumptions about the data. The data does not have to be interval or be normally distributed.

Parametric tests

T-tests

These tests compare the means of two samples and determine if the probability of any difference between them have been obtained by chance. Either a one-tailed or two-tailed test can be applied, depending on the result that your hypothesis. For example, if your hypothesis predicts that the mean age of women in a particular industry is lower than that of men, a T-test can be performed to check if the observed difference in mean age is unlikely to have occurred by chance.

In Excel you would use the 'TTEST' worksheet function. In SPSS, the T-test command is found under 'Compare Means' in the 'Statistics' menu. There are two types of T-test you are likely to need to use.

Paired sample

This is essentially a before and after scenario. For example, you may want to assess the effectiveness of a training programme on the length of time it takes to perform a task. Table 9.3 shows the times recorded before and after training of twelve workers.

Worker	Before	After
1	18.00	14.00
2	19.00	12.00
3	14.00	10.00
4	16.00	12.00
5	12.00	8.00
6	18.00	10.00
7	16.00	10.00
8	18.00	8.00
9	16.00	12.00
10	19.00	16.00
11	16.00	14.00
12	16.00	12.00

Table 9.3. A paired sample.

In every case, training has reduced the time taken to perform a task. This appears pretty conclusive in that the training programme does appear to have increased the speed of carrying out the task, but the number of trainees is small and it may well be the result of chance or sampling error.

Using the 'TTEST' function in Excel, or the 'Paired-Samples T-test' in SPSS, the probability of this occurring by chance is less than 0.001, using the one-tailed test of significance. In other words, it is very unlikely that this set of observations is the result of chance. The training appears to be an effective one.

To have more confidence in this finding, you would also set up a parallel, or 'control', group of workers who do not receive training, but are tested on the same occasions. You can then check that the reduction in time is not also due to familiarity as a result of having carried out the task before.

Independent samples
The second type of T-test you are likely to need to use involves a comparison of means of a variable for two independent samples. The aim is to see if the two samples are likely to have been drawn from two different populations, or from the same population.

▶ *Example* – You wish to compare the mean salaries of male and female workers. You would use the **independent sample T-test** to compare the means of each sample and determine if they are statistically significant.

There is a slight complication in this technique relating to the **variance** of the values in each group. You will recall from chapter 8 that variance is a measure of the spread of values in a sample, and can be calculated from the **standard deviation**. There are two variants of the independent samples T-test. One assumes that there is no statistically significant difference between the variances of the two samples; the second assumes there is a significant difference. This is determined using a test of variance called the **F-test.**

In SPSS, the F-test is automatically applied when you run the independent samples T-test. The output provides you with a range of measures including the result of an F-test. It will tell you whether or not the variance is statistically significant. It will also provide you with both versions of the T-test results. You choose the appropriate result according to whether or not the difference in variance is statistically significant. In Excel, it is a little more complicated. You must run the 'FTEST' function that will determine the one-tailed significance of the difference in variance between the two samples, before carrying out the T-test.

Table 9.4 records the times taken by 12 male and 12 female workers in performing a task.

The FTEST in Excel shows that the one-tailed statistical significance of the difference in variance between male and female workers, in the time taken to perform a particular task, is actually $p = 0.6$. In other words, it is not significant, and the level of diversity in times is very similar in males and females. You can now apply the correct version of the TTEST function to test the hypothesis that there is a statistically significant difference between males and females.

The result of a T-test in Excel shows significance at $p < 0.001$, in other words very significant. In this sample, the male workers clearly demonstrated that they were slower on average than females in this task, and the difference is statistically significant. However, the general spread of times within each gender group shows no statistically significant difference.

Of course, the sample is very small. However, the level of

Subject	Males	Females		
1	18.00	14.00	Range:	
2	19.00	12.00	Male	7.00 seconds
3	14.00	10.00	Female	8.00 seconds
4	16.00	12.00		
5	12.00	8.00		
6	18.00	10.00	Mean Times:	
7	16.00	10.00	Male	16.50 seconds
8	18.00	8.00	Female	11.50 seconds
9	16.00	12.00		
10	19.00	16.00		
11	16.00	14.00		
12	16.00	12.00		

Table 9.4. Applying the F-test.

significance is very high, making it worth investigating this effect in more detail.

If you use SPSS to perform the T-test, the result would be as shown in table 9.5.

As is often the case with SPSS printouts, there is much information that the inexperienced eye finds difficult to interpret. The F-test shows no statistical significance (i.e. $p = 0.54$ that there is no real difference in variance) and so *equal variances are assumed*. The T-test under these circumstances shows that the difference in means is statistically significant ($p < 0.001$). The '95% confidence interval of the difference' indicates a 95% probability that the true difference in means between the two groups lies between 3.09 and 6.91 (rounded to two decimal places).

Non-parametric tests

Chi-square (x^2)

This is a good general-purpose non-parametric test. The test involves comparing the observed frequencies of each category against the frequencies that you would have expected to observe if the *null hypothesis* were correct. The test generates the probability that the

		Levene's Test for Equality of Variances		t-test for Equality of Means					95% Confidence Interval of the Difference	
		F	Sig.	t	df	Sig (2-tailed)	Mean Difference	Std. Error Difference	Lower	Upper
TIME	Equal variances assumed	.388	.540	5.428	22	.000	5.0000	.9211	3.0897	6.9103
	Equal varianes not assumed			5.428	21.466	.000	5.0000	.9211	3.0868	6.9132

Table 9.5. Independent samples text.

observed frequencies could have been obtained by chance – i.e. probability that the null hypothesis is correct.

SPSS will generate the chi-square statistic very easily, calculating the expected frequencies automatically. In Excel, you will need to work out the expected frequencies for yourself. Table 9.6 shows a table drawn up from the responses to a question summarised by gender.

Observed frequencies		Male	Female	Totals
	Yes	100	500	600
	Neutral	50	70	120
	No	150	750	900
	Totals	300	1320	
Expected frequencies		Male	Female	Totals
	Yes	111.1	488.9	600
	Neutral	22.2	97.8	120
	No	166.7	733.3	900
	Totals	300	1320	

Table 9.6. Applying the chi-square test.

The **observed frequencies** table is created directly from the questionnaire responses and is generated using the **pivot tables** facility in Excel. The **expected frequencies** have to be calculated in accordance with the ratios of the distribution in the table. If there is no real difference in the responses of male and female respondents, the ratio of YES, NEUTRAL and NO will be the same for both genders (i.e. in the ratio of 600:120:900). You need to distribute the 300 males and 1320 females between the three possible responses in that ratio. In other words, if there is no real difference between the genders, the distribution of their responses will be the same.

Use the CHITEST function in Excel. In SPSS, the chi-test is found in the 'Statistics' menu under the 'Non-parametric tests' option.

▶ *Caution* – Small numbers present a problem with this test. If any of the cells of data have an expected value of less than 5, you need to use this test with caution. However, you can be less cautious if there are more than three categories involved in the test. The rule of thumb to adopt is that if 20% or more of the expected frequencies are less than 5, or any are less than 1, the chi-square test should not be used like this. You should regroup the data (see chapter 7) so that the expected frequencies of grouped categories satisfy these requirements. Clearly, you will need to modify your hypothesis so that it relates to the grouped categories rather than the original ones. For example, if you have four categories of ethnic groups, but the numbers are low, you may have to regroup them into a single dichotomous variable, such as 'white European' and 'Others'.

Footnote: degrees of freedom

Both Excel and SPSS will calculate the degrees of freedom during the data processing. However, for the sake of completeness the following method is used for determining degrees of freedom with tables of data:

degrees of freedom = (number of rows 1) x (number of columns 1)

In the example above (table 9.5), there are 2 degrees of freedom:

$$Df = (3-1) \times (2-1) = 2 \times 1 = 2$$

Tutorial: helping you learn

Progress questions

1. When exploring causal relationships, how do the terms 'spurious', 'intervening' and 'interacting variables' explain possible errors?

2. What is meant by a 'test of statistical significance'?

2. What are the main assumptions that underpin (a) parametric and (b) non-parametric tests of significance?

3. Under what circumstances would you use a (a) one-tailed test, and (b) two-tailed test of significance?

4. What is a T-test designed to test the significance of? How is an F-test related to it?

5. Chi-square is a good general test for use with nominal and ordinal data. What is the test comparing to arrive at a judgement about statistical significance?

Discussion points

In an attempt to minimise the risk of committing a Type I error, a researcher decides to use $p < 0.01$ rather than 0.05 as the test for rejecting the null hypothesis. By doing so, though, the researcher increases the risk of committing a Type II error. Discuss why that is the case. In what circumstances do you think a Type II error is preferable to a Type I error?

Assignment

The web site accompanying this book has examples of frequency tables and data sets on the page for this chapter. Develop hypotheses about the relationships between variables and use Excel, SPSS or other appropriate software application to test those hypotheses. Justify any decision for rejecting or accepting the null hypotheses and assess the risks associated with making Type I and Type II errors.

Study tips

Research papers that present statistical analyses will also show the statistical justification (in other words, tests of statistical significance). When you read these papers and articles, note how the reseacher(s) often identifies the importance of such information when arguing a case. You will need to develop this sort of approach yourself, when presenting statistical evidence in support of any hypotheses you put forward.

10

Exploring Bivariate Analysis

One-minute Overview – Bivariate analysis is concerned with exploring the strength of a relationship between two variables. This can be shown in reports and articles as summary data presented in bivariate (contingency) tables, to show the broad relationship between the dependent and independent variables. The strength of the relationship is measured using the technique of correlation. This measures the degree of association as a correlation coefficient, using a scale ranging from $+1$ to $^-1$, i.e. positive and negative correlation. Pearson's product moment (Pearson's r) is the coefficient used where both variables are interval. Spearman's rho measures correlation where one of the variables at least is ordinal. Phi is used where at least one variable is nominal and dichotomous. If the relationship is linear, the correlation high and statistically significant, linear regression can be used to generate a formula to predict the value of the dependent variable for any given value of the independent variable. Plotting a scatter graph with a trendline will help you identify whether or not the relationship is linear, or nearly so. In this chapter we will explore:

▶ bivariate analysis
▶ bivariate (or contingency) tables
▶ creating the variable categories
▶ the strength of a relationship: correlation
▶ linear regression

Bivariate analysis

Chapter 9 discussed ways of identifying the probability of a real relationship between two variables. This chapter looks at how you might quantify that relationship, and measure its strength. This approach is called **bivariate analysis**. There are several ways of measuring the strength of these relationships. Both Excel and SPSS are good software packages to use. Indeed, the complexity of the calculations makes them invaluable. SPSS is better at the task because it was specifically designed for it.

Bivariate (or contingency) tables

Known also as **cross-tabulations**, you will often see **bivariate tables** of data in textbooks and journal papers. They present complex data about two variables in a way that summarises them in a form that shows a relationship in a much better way than any frequency table can. Table 10.1 is an example.

	Gender	
	Male	Female
High self-esteem	66.7%	45%
	300	(225)
Low self-esteem	33.3%	55%
	(100)	(275)

$$N = 900$$
$$p < 0.05$$
$$Phi = 0.3$$

Table 10.1. A cross-tabulation (bivariate table) of imaginary data.

This table summarises the observed relationship between two dichotomous variables – self-esteem and gender – within an imaginary sample of respondents to a questionnaire. On the basis of this table, the obvious hypothesis is that men are more likely to have higher self-esteem than women.

There are several features of the table that should be explained. N = 900 represents the total number of respondents in the sample. It is essential to include this so that your readers know how large the sample was, an important question when assessing the quality of your results. The numbers in brackets represent the actual numbers of respondents in each category of the table (called a cell). Data in a cross-tabulation can be presented as percentages or absolute numbers, and it is good to use both.

P < 0.05 represents the level of statistical significance. In this case it is at the limit of acceptability. Phi = 0.3 represents the **correlation coefficient**, the strength of the association between these two variables. This measure is explained in more detail later in the chapter. All three measures are important and need to be shown as it helps the reader to make an assessment of the validity of your argument.

Dependent and independent variables

The placing of a variable (i.e. as rows or columns) is, by convention, quite important. The **dependent variable** makes up the rows and the **independent variable** makes up the columns. The hypothesis explored in table 10.1 is that self-esteem is dependent on (i.e. influenced by) gender. Self-esteem is the dependent variable. Gender is the independent variable.

Creating the variable categories

Each variable in table 10.1 is a dichotomy. While this is always going to be the case with some variables, such as gender, it is not always so with many others. In table 10.1, for example, the self-esteem variable may be an ordinal measure, or it could be a scale or index that approaches the interval level of measurement.

The bivariate table differs from a straight frequency table in that variables are often collapsed into a very limited number of groups (rarely more than two or three) to show relationships in broad terms. Therefore, a cut-off value is needed to mark the boundary between high and low. This could be taken as the median value. So, if self-esteem is measured on a scale of 1 to 10, the median value of 5.5 might be the cut-off value. All scores above 5.5 might be regarded as high, and all those up to 5.5 interpreted as low.

Again, here is a situation where software packages take the drudge out of the task. In SPSS, in the *Transform* menu, you would use the *Recode* command to create a new derived variable based on the cut-off value. Values up to 5.5 might be recoded as 1 (i.e. low), and all those above 5.5 recoded as 2 (i.e. high). To play safe, you can instruct the program to generate a new variable using these new values, and it is these that are cross-tabulated with gender using the *Statistics* > *Summarise* > *Crosstabs* commands in the menu bar. In setting up the cross-tabulation, you can select the statistical tests shown in table 10.1 (i.e. chi-square and correlation).

In Excel, this task is rather more difficult. The values can be recoded using the IF function, and a cross-tabulation created through the use of **pivot tables,** but the process is not as elegant as that carried out by SPSS. Frankly, once you reach the stage of having to present data in this way, a good statistical package like SPSS becomes invaluable. Of course, the task can be done manually, which is fine if the number of cases (respondents) is not enormous. The calculation of chi-square was described in the last chapter, and this should present no problems in either SPSS or Excel, but the correlation coefficient the strength of the relationship needs to be explained.

The strength of a relationship: correlation

The degree of association between two variables is quite important in attempting to describe how close the link is between the two. For example, if your hypothesis states that the level of self-esteem is linked to gender, then in the perfect relationship between the two, all males would show high self-esteem and all females would show low self-esteem. In other words there would be perfect correlation. In reality this perfection is extremely rare in the social sciences, as explained in chapter 9. There are always likely to be other factors involved. The idea of correlation helps us identify the degree to which one variable influences another.

Figure 10.1 illustrates correlation.

▶ 10.1a shows the distribution of cases plotted on a graph. They are clustered closely together around a straight line, indicating a strong relationship between the values on one variable with the value on another.

▶ 10.1b also shows a strong correlation, but it is in the negative direction. In other words, as the independent variable increases, the dependent variable decreases.

▶ 10.1c shows no correlation whatsoever. The plots are scattered all over the place, without any pattern to their distribution.

This type of graph is called a scatter graph, and this will be described shortly.

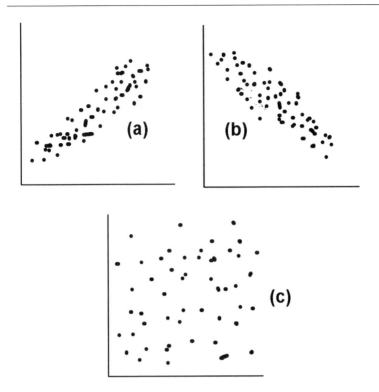

Figure 10.1. An illustration of correlation.

Correlation is represented numerically as a decimal ranging from ‾1 to +1. This is called the correlation coefficient. +1 and ‾1 represent perfect correlation, while zero means there is no correlation whatsoever.

Rarely is any one variable totally dependent on another. Other factors have an effect that moderates the relationship between any two variables, so the relationship is less than perfect. For example, the correlation coefficient may be +0.6, still positive; in other words both variables increase with each other.

Examples

It is worth spending a moment or two looking at hypothetical examples to illustrate what this means in real life.

1. If you were to examine the rate of spending on primary phase education and the effect this had on the SATs results at age eleven,

you would look at the correlation between the two (as well as its statistical significance). It is likely that this will show a positive correlation, but this is unlikely to be perfect. A **correlation coefficient** of +0.6 would be quite strong in view of the other likely social and economic factors that will play their part. A correlation coefficient of +0.1 is very low and will make you question the wisdom of throwing so much money at the problem.

2. Another example to illustrate **negative correlation** might be the effect of increasing police investment in supporting their local community in setting up and maintaining Neighbourhood Watch schemes. A test of this investment would be the effect on property-related crime. Here, you would be looking for a strong negative correlation. As investment was increased, you would expect property-related crime to decrease. Again, you would be looking for a strong negative value (e.g. −0.7).

Scatter graphs

Chapter 7 looked at ways of summarising your research data in ways that allowed you to get a 'feel' for what is going on in general. When you are looking at the effect of one variable on another, a scatter graph is a useful way of displaying data that gives an overall impression of the relationship. You can only use this approach when both variables are **interval**. If one or both variables are **ordinal** but have a large number of categories (e.g. a scale or index) it is acceptable to use this method of displaying the data.

Figure 10.2 shows a **scatter graph** generated from data collected as part of a survey of mature students on Access courses. Each of the small stars represents the data from one respondent (case). It plots the age of the respondent by how long it has been since the respondent was in formal study.

As you might expect, there is a general dispersion of the plots, but there is a general trend of **positive correlation** between respondent age and the length of time it has been since previous formal study. The straight sloping line is called a **regression line** and is the 'best guess' prediction line – i.e. it provides a visual display of the degree of correlation.

Both SPSS and Excel will generate scatter graphs and insert the regression line. In SPSS, the graph is created from the *Graphs* command. In Excel use the chart wizard to create the graph.

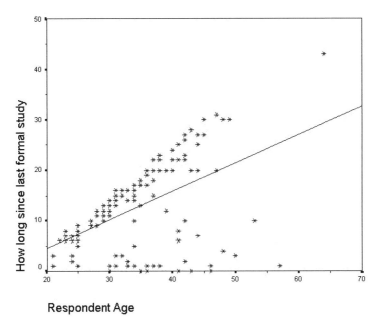

Figure 10.2. A scatter graph.

Selecting *Add Trendline* adds the regression line from the *Chart* command on the menu bar. This is done after the graph has been generated.

Correlation coefficients
While the scatter graph will provide a useful visual idea of correlation, you will also want to quantify it. The correlation coefficient can be calculated in SPSS and Excel. First, you need to describe the different types of coefficient you are likely to use, depending on the type of variables you are working with.

Interval data
The **Pearson's product moment correlation coefficient** (shortened to 'Pearson's r') is used. This statistic assumes that both variables are interval, and that the relationship between them is linear. The scatter graph and its trend line will indicate this.

In SPSS, Pearson's r is calculated from the *Statistics* command. Select *Bivariate* from the *Correlate* option within the *Statistics* command. Here you can choose a one- or two-tailed test of significance. It is important to use this, as it is possible that your result is not statistically significant, with all that implies. The output from this command will look something like table 10.2.

		Respondent age	How long since last formal study?
Respondent age	Pearson correlation	1.000	.500
	Sig. (1-tailed)		P < .000
	N	139	135
	N	139	135
How long since last formal study?	Pearson correlation	.500	1.000
	Sig. (1-tailed)	P < .000	
	N	135	138
	N	135	138

Table 10.2. Pearson's r for data on access students' last formal study.

SPSS always creates a matrix in which all the selected variables are cross-tabulated against each other. Obviously, a variable matched against itself will always yield a coefficient of 1. The Pearson's r for age and formal study is +0.5. The predicted direction would be positive so the one-tailed significance measure is invoked, and it is highly significant at p < 0.001. Note the discrepancy in N, the number of respondents included. This is because the calculations exclude cases where the data is missing.

In Excel, the Pearson's r is calculated using the Pearson function and entering the two arrays of data. The output is a single figure for Pearson's r. You will need to apply a test of significance separately (e.g. CHITEST). Also, in Excel, you may want to use **Add-ins**. These are extra functions available for specific purposes. One of these Add-ins is for statistical analysis. To install them onto your computer, select the *Tools* menu and *Add-ins*. Follow the instructions to install the *Analysis Toolpak* (this is the correct spelling!). You will now have direct access to a number of analytical tools through the *Data Analysis* command in the *Tools* menu. The correlation tool will generate a correlation matrix as shown in table 10.2.

Ordinal data

A different measure of correlation is recommended for ordinal measures. This is called **Spearman's rho**. It makes fewer assumptions about the data. It works by comparing the rankings (order) of the variable values, rather than comparing the interval differences.

In SPSS, you can specify Spearman's rho when you ask the program to set up a bivariate correlation matrix as described above. The result is interpreted in much the same way as for Pearson's r because the statistic means the same thing to all intents and purposes. Excel does not calculate Spearman's rho.

Dichotomous nominal data

The value of the correlation coefficient is really seen with interval data. After all, it is a measure of the relationship between values that are changing. Spearman's rho does address the need to examine this relationship with ordinal values. There is also a measure that looks at the strength of the relationship between dichotomous nominal variables (e.g. Gender, Yes/No, etc). This is called Phi and is the measure shown in table 10.1. SPSS will calculate Phi as part of the *Crosstabs* command in the *Statistics* menu.

Selecting the best measure

So far, the descriptions of correlation coefficients assume that your variables are of the same type. This is not always so. You may need to compare interval with ordinal, ordinal with dichotomous, or interval with dichotomous. Adopt the measure that relates to the lowest level of measure. If for example you are comparing interval with ordinal, you will use Spearman's rho.

Rule of thumb interpretation: the coefficient of determination (R square)

The correlation coefficient has a valuable role in estimating what proportion of variance in the dependent variable is explained by the variance in the independent variable. The square of the correlation coefficient gives you the proportion of variance explained. The value is called the **coefficient of determination**.

For example, in table 10.2, the correlation between mature students' ages and the length of time it has been since their previous experience of formal education is 0.5. Squaring this (i.e. 0.5 x 0.5) gives you 0.25. In other words, 25% of the variance in the length of time since last formal study can be explained by respondents' age. This leaves 75% of the variance unexplained – there are other factors at play there. This is the subject of chapter 11.

We can talk about weak, moderate and strong correlations. A rule of thumb is that positive or negative correlations below 0.2 are very low, between 0.2 and 0.40 low, 0.4 to 0.7 moderate, 0.7 to 0.9 high, and anything above this very high.

Curvilinear relationship: an added complication

Everything described so far in this chapter assumes a linear relationship between variables. In other words, a graph that plots the variables will yield something approaching a straight line. But this is not always so, and a scatter graph may seem to show that the regression line is actually a curve. When that happens, you cannot use correlation coefficients because they relate to linear relationships. The answer, then, is to find a relationship that is linear so that correlation can be applied. It is important to plot scatter graphs precisely for the reason of being able to judge whether there is a linear or near linear relationship. Only then can you apply correlation statistics.

A way of approaching that problem is to plot the dependent variable against the **log of the independent variable**. The effect is often to generate a linear, or at least near linear, relationship. Figure 10.3 shows this. Figure 10.3a is the scatter graph of the variables showing a very clear curve in the negative direction. If the values for the independent variable are converted to their logarithms, figure 10.3b is the result. There now appears to be a linear relationship between the dependent variable and the log of the independent variable. Pearson's r can now be calculated for that relationship.

Linear regression

The idea of a **regression line** was discussed earlier. It is the straight line drawn on the scatter graph that best fits the plotted points. This line can be described by a general mathematical formula for a straight-line graph:

$$y = mx + c$$

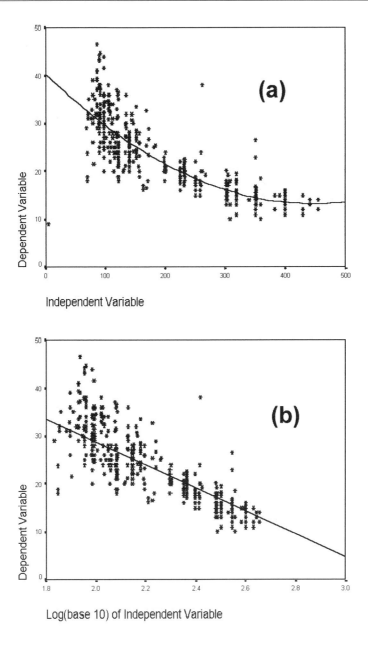

Figure. 10.3. Plotting the dependent variable against the log of the independent vairable.

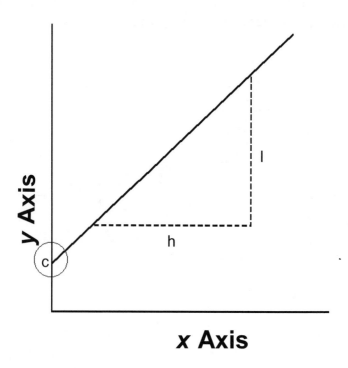

Figure 10.4. A hypothetical regression line.

Figure 10.4 shows a hypothetical regression line that will help explain the equation above.

'*y*' is the value on the '*y*' axis

'*x*' is the value on the '*x*' ('*c*', the intercept, is the point where the line cuts the '*y*' axis)

'*m*' is the gradient or slope of the line and measures the degree of steepness as shown by the dotted triangle, calculated by dividing the value of '*h*' by the value of '*l*'.

From this formula we can calculate, or predict, the value of '*y*' for any known value of '*x*' even if that point is not plotted on the graph. For example, if we know that '*m*' equals 0.5 and '*c*' equals 10, it is easy to predict the value of '*y*' when '*x*' equals 15:

$$'y' = (0.5 \times 15) + 10 = 17.5$$

This is the purpose of linear regression. It attempts to create a mathematical formula based on that shown above, that can then be used for prediction. As you might guess, this method can only be carried out on interval data. SPSS and Excel will create linear regressions.

▶ In EXCEL – use the *Regression* command found in the *Tools > Data Analysis* commands from the menu bar.

▶ In SPSS – use the *Statistics* menu and its *Regression > Linear* sub-command. Table 10.3 shows the output generated by SPSS for the mature students on Access courses. It looks at the relationship between age and the last time they were in formal study.

Model		Unstandardised coefficients		Standardised coefficients	t	Sig.
		B	Standard error	Beta		
1	(Constant)	-6.575	3.019		-2.178	.031
	Q1 Age	.561	.084	.500	6.657	.000

Table 10.3. Linear regression.

The regression equation for the line that will predict the number of years since a respondent of a particular age was in formal education is:

$$time = (0.561 \times age) \ ^{-}6.575$$

For someone aged 40, the predicted absence from formal education is fractionally under 16 years (15.9). The problem is that the database had four respondents aged 40 and the actual absence for them was 20 years for two, and 22 and 24 respectively for the remaining two. This is quite a large discrepancy.

Linear regression is on very dubious ground when the correlation between the two variables concerned is low. If you examine figure 10.2, you can see why this is so. There is a large cluster of cases that appear to run in a straight line placed above the regression line on the chart, but there are cases scattered all over the place below this line, creating a form of 'noise' resulting from factors other than age. In fact, you can see that quite a few respondents across the age spectrum have had very recent experience of formal education. This has depressed the slope of the regression line. Linear regression should only be applied when correlation is high.

▶ Remember the effect of **outliers** on the dataset (chapter 7).

Note also, that the constant and the 'age' multiplier are subject to standard error. In other words, the constant may range from −3.556 to −9.594. Similarly, the age multiplier may range from 0.645 to 0.477. The standard errors are quite large and make it difficult to produce a reasonably accurate prediction.

The relationship between and purpose of correlation and linear regression is very close, but their roles are different. Correlation is concerned with measuring the strength of the relationship between two variables and, by calculating the coefficient of determination, determining the proportion of variance in the dependent variable caused by the independent variable. If the correlation is high to very high, the use of linear regression can be justified as a method of creating an equation to predict a value of the dependent variable. All this assumes, of course, that the relationship is statistically significant at least to $p < 0.05$.

Tutorial: helping you learn

Progress questions

1. What is the relationship between correlation and linear regression?

2. If you were exploring the correlation between gender and salary levels in a certain industry, should you use Pearson's r, Phi, or Spearman's rho correlation coefficient?

3. The correlation coefficient of two variables is found to be −0.3. Would linear regression be an appropriate method to use to predict likely values of the independent variable? Give reasons for your answer.

4. Why do you plot a scatter graph before attempting to calculate correlation coefficients or linear regression formulae?

Discussion points

Since the real value of linear regression lies in generating a formula that allows you to predict possible values of a dependent variable, discuss possible applications of this approach in the applied social sciences.

Assignment

The web site that accompanies this book contains datasets on the page for this chapter. Download the data and examine each dataset for relationships between the variables. In particular, plot a scatter graph to make a visual assessment of linear association and then generate a correlation coefficient for this association. Compare the scatter graphs with the correlation coefficients to see how the distribution of the plots is associated with the strength of the coefficients. Is it valid to use linear regression to create predictions? If it is valid for any dataset, carry out linear regression and then test the predictions made from it against actual values in the dataset.

Study tips

Sociology and psychology textbooks are a good source of examples of bivariate tables and descriptions of relationships between variables. Look at how the writers have constructed their tables and also taken care (we hope!) with reporting the statistical measures associated with them. Identify where there is good practice in reporting this data and follow their example. Also, examine the statistics presented in detail and question, where appropriate, the claims made for the data on the basis of the strength of association.

11

Multivariate Analysis

One-minute Overview – The statistical relationship between two variables is rarely perfectly causal. The coefficient of determination will make that very clear. One of the easiest ways of testing for complex relationships is to generate a correlation matrix of all the non-nominal variables, and look for moderate to high correlation coefficients. Where several variables are strongly correlated to each other, use partial correlation to remove the effect of one of these variables and see if there is any change in the correlation between your dependent and other independent variables. If there is an obvious reduction, this may mean that it is an intervening or moderating variable. Use multiple regression to identify the relative importance of each independent variable, and/or to predict values of your dependent variable for any given set of independent variable values. It is usually better to present findings of this kind as a bivariate table showing the effect of the control variable(s). In this chapter we will explore:

▶ multivariate analysis
▶ partial correlation
▶ multiple regression
▶ using control variables in bivariate tables

Multivariate analysis

In chapter 10 the discussion focused on the relationship between two variables and the methods of assessing strength of association. In chapter 9, though, it was pointed out that life is rarely so simple. When exploring the factors that influence a particular variable, we usually need to look at a range of variables and how they may interact to affect the dependent variable. The idea of 'intervening' and 'interacting' variables was introduced in that chapter. Therefore, in building up your hypothesis and testing it, you will explore how variables are linked to each other. This is called **multivariate analysis**.

The techniques are essentially similar to those described in chapter 10, but more complex. Try to use a dedicated statistics package like SPSS for this work. However, Excel can undertake some of the tasks described in this chapter.

Partial correlation

Before exploring potential relationships between all the variables in your data, do the individual variable checks described in chapters 7 and 8. Check the data for errors and outliers, generate summary statistics, and test for normality of distribution. Then make any appropriate adjustments. Bear in mind, though, that changing or removing data from your analysis is something to consider very carefully. It must be fully justified if you are not to face criticism. Then you can follow the procedure described below:

1. Construct a correlation matrix of all the variables to see if there are any statistically significant correlations.

2. Look for strong relationships and explore these by developing hypotheses that you can test. For example, is the relationship between gender and self-esteem (see the hypothetical example in chapter 10), which is statistically significant, actually modified or moderated by age? (e.g. are self-esteem differences between genders affected by respondent age?).

3. Carry out a partial correlation where the correlation between the dependent and independent variables in your hypothesis are compared, before and after the effects of other variables are accounted for.

If the strength of association (and its statistical significance) remains the same (or very nearly so) after this, then the **controlling variables**, as they are called, are not intervening or moderating ones. If, however, the correlation between the variables is weakened after accounting for age, then that indicates a moderating effect of the third variable (e.g. age). Of course the correlation, or its statistical significance, may fall very dramatically. In this case you would need to question whether or not the association was spurious.

This is where social statistics become really interesting. You are now actively engaged in testing ideas about potentially complex relationships between quantitative variables. The following hypothetical example shows how this works.

Example

As part of a study of employees in a company, a researcher collects data on salary levels, educational attainment, and level within the organisation of those employees who have been with the company for 5 years. The researcher finds a high correlation between starting salary and current salary, as shown in table 11.1.

	Gender	Educational attainment	Job level	Current salary	Start salary
Gender	1				
Educational attainment	-0.36*	1			
Job level	-0.38*	0.52*	1		
Current salary	-0.45*	0.67*	0.79*	1	
Start salary	-0.46*	0.64*	0.76*	0.90*	1

Table 11.1. A correlation matrix of variables in a survey of 550 employees. $p < 0.01$ Correlations that do not have an * against them are not statistically significant.

Current and starting salaries are also significantly correlated with gender, educational attainment and job level. The important question to ask is: do any of these variables have a causal relationship? **Partial correlation** will help to answer that question.

The technique uses the approach of calculating the **correlation coefficient** between the independent and dependent variables after the effect of one or more other variables (the **control variables**) are accounted for, in other words the proportion of correlation contributed by the control variable. You then compare the answer with the original correlation coefficient to see if the value has been reduced.

In SPSS, the command is *Statistics* > *Correlation* > *Partial* from the menu bar. The dependent and independent variables are selected as is also a control variable. You can select more than one control variable, but using one at a time allows you to check the effect of each individual variable. The one- or two-tailed test of significance needs to be selected as appropriate.

Table 11.2 shows the partial correlation matrices generated using the three control variables: gender, educational attainment, and job level.

1. Controlling for gender

	Current salary	Start salary
Current salary	1	
Start salary	0.85	1
	$p < 0.01$	

2. Controlling for educational attainment

	Current salary	Start salary
Current salary	1	
Start salary	0.80	1
	$p < 0.01$	

3. Controlling for job level

	Current salary	Start salary
Current salary	1	
Start salary	0.71	1
	$p < 0.01$	

Table 11.2. Partial correlation tables.

Gender has a small effect, but educational attainment and especially job level have marked effects on the correlation between current and starting salaries. If both variables are 'controlled for', the correlation between current and start salaries reduces to 0.63, with $p < 0.01$. In other words, both job level and educational attainment have a moderating effect on salary progression. This allows for possible interpretations to be explored.

For example, one possible interpretation is that salary progression is closely linked to job level in that salary progression can be achieved mainly through promotion. The link with educational attainment might be through the twin tracks of recruitment and promotion. For example, managers are more likely to have stayed in education for longer, perhaps to gain a degree or appropriate vocational qualifications, and may have been recruited at higher levels. At the same time, though, managers are also promoted into this level because of organisational career structures. In such cases, staff may not have the same level of educational attainment. The evidence is in the smaller controlling effect of educational attainment on the correlation between start and current salaries.

The data has resulted in the hypothesis described in the last paragraph. It has not proved this but simply provides evidence to generate a hypothesis that now needs to be tested in some other way (such as in-depth interviews).

Multiple regression

As discussed in chapter 10, correlation can point to statistically significant relationships between variables, but it cannot make predictions. This is the role of **regression. Multiple regression** is a technique for examining how far independent variables contribute to predicting the quantity of the dependent variable. The assumptions governing the use of this technique are rather like those described for linear regression in chapter 10. The key assumptions are that the data is interval in nature, and that the relationship between them is linear.

Multiple regression will generate an equation to predict the value of the dependent variable from all the statistically significantly correlated independent variables. In the social sciences there is probably less call for this technique except in those areas of social policy linked to economics or provision of resources that generate the social infrastructure (growth in demand for housing, transport, health services). As with linear regression, the nature of the subjects (human populations) makes the predictive ability of this technique something to be cautious about. All the same, it does produce a mathematical model that provides us with useful information about what is likely to happen when the contributing variables are accounted for – assuming the statistician is aware of all the variables and has recorded them accurately.

SPSS carries out multiple regression very efficiently from the *Statistics* > *Regression* > *Linear* menu. The method of setting up the regression is slightly different to that described in chapter 10. You enter all the independent variables to be tested, and then choose a method of calculating the statistics. There are several methods, but the two most used methods are:

1. ENTER: The effect of all the independent variables is calculated as a single group. Each variable is entered into the calculation in descending order of influence. This means that the most influential variable appears first, and the least influential variable last.

2. STEPWISE: The effect of each individual variable is calculated and the results displayed before the next variable is entered.

In the case of STEPWISE method, the variables will be entered only if its effect results in a model that is statistically significant. SPSS will stop the calculation if this ceiling is reached, even if there are more variables to be handled. The reason is obvious. There is little point in calculating a model if the end result has no statistical significance. It is for this reason that the STEPWISE method is popular.

Table 11.3 is the model summary generated by SPSS in the salary study.

The SPSS printout is pretty complex, but this table of data is the one to concentrate on. Gender was included in the specification for the analysis, but not during calculation, because its effect was not found to be statistically significant. Multiple regression has created three possible mathematical models for predicting an employee's salary. Model 1 includes the most important influencing factor (i.e. start salary) and a prediction based purely on this model would be (rounding coefficients to 1 decimal place):

Coefficients(0					
Model	Unstandardised coefficients		Standardised coefficients Beta	t	Sig.
	B	Std. Error			
1　(Constant) 　　Start salary	1928.206 1.909	888.680 .047	.880	2.170 40.276	.031 .000
2　(Constant) 　　Start salary 　　Employment level	1036.931 1.469 5947.000	832.051 .067 683.430	.677 .269	1.246 21.873 8.702	.213 .000 .000
3　(Constant) 　　Start salary 　　Employment level 　　Educational 　　attainment (years)	-7786.970 1.274 5.657.018 929.264	1632.558 .072 659.427 149.823	.587 .256 .157	-4.770 17.749 8.579 6.202	.000 .000 .000 .000

Table 11.3. Multiple regression: a salary study.

Current salary = 1.9 (Start salary) + 1928.2

This is based on the $y = mx + c$ equation discussed in chapter 10.
Model 2 predicts current salary as:

= [1.5 (Start salary)] + [5947 (Employment level)] + 1036.9

Model 3 predicts current salary as:

= [1.3 (Start salary)] + [5657 (Employment level)] + [929.3
(Educational attainment)] −7787

Of course, the system of modelling depends on so many factors. There is the reliability of your research design and, of course a presumption that all possible variables have been taken into account. So, any predictions based on this type of modelling require cautious acceptance.

Also included in a regression output about coefficients is information on the standard error of these values. It would be good practice to use this to determine the 95% confidence limits of the coefficient values, and so calculate the 95% confidence limits of predicted range of current salaries. This will probably yield a 'safe' zone of prediction.

There are two other key pieces of information to be gleaned from this type of analysis. The first is the order of introducing the variables into the regression. This is in descending order of importance: Start salary > Job level > Educational attainment. This helps to support the hypothesis described earlier. For this feature alone, multiple regression is a useful tool. The second piece of information is the coefficient of determination. Table 11.4 shows this (R square) for each of the three models.

Model	R	R square	Adjusted R square	Standard error of the estimate
1	.880(a)	.775	.774	£8,115.36
2	.898(b)	.806	.805	£7,540.43
3	.906(c)	.821	.819	£7,257.28

Table 11.4. Coefficient of determination: salary study.

(a) Predictors: (constant), start salary
(b) Predictors: (constant), start salary, employment level
(c) Predictors: (constant), start salary, employment level, educational attainment (years)

Model 1 explains 77% of the variance in current salary; Model 2 explains 80% and Model 3 explains 82%. This still leaves 18% of variance that must be explained by other factors. All the same, a coefficient of determination this high is quite good.

Using control variables in bivariate tables

The problem with multiple regression is that it is not a particularly comprehensible way of reporting your findings. By far the best way is to use bivariate tables as described in chapter 10. Multiple regression shows what variables are important and points to how they might be reported. Again, you can turn to SPSS to create your tables to show the effect of a third variable on the dependent variable. Table 11.5 shows how to produce a table showing the relationship between start salary and current salary controlled for the effect of employment level.

Start salary			Employment level			
			Low		High	
			Start salary			
	Low	High	Low	High	Low	High
Current Low salary	76.5% (202)	17.1% (36)	80.1% (202)	31.3% (35)	7.7% (1)	1.0% (1)
High	23.5% (62)	82.9% (174)	19.9% (50)	68.8% (77)	92.3% (12)	99.0% (97)
	$p < 0.001$ Phi = 0.59 (N = 474)		$p < 0.001$ Phi = 0.47 (N - 363)		Not significant Phi - 0.16 (N = 111)	

Table 11.5. Cross-tabulation of current salary and
starting salary controlled for job level.

The interpretation of this table is complicated by the fact that one
of the sub-tables shows no statistical significance, but the overall
interpretation will go something like this:

1. The low and high cut-off values for salary were their respective
    median values of £15,000 for start salary, and £29,000 for current
    salary. It is important to remember that low and high are not the
    same value ranges for the two sets of salaries. The cut-off point for
    job level was low = clerical staff; high = supervisors and
    managers.

2. Taking the extreme left-hand sub-table, it is clear that those
    employees who began on a low salary were three times less likely to
    have progressed to the high category in their current salaries.
    Those whose starting salaries were within the high range were now
    about four times more likely to be receiving salaries in the high
    range of current salaries. This is not surprising. You would expect
    someone starting on a high salary to continue to maintain a
    differential over time. The fact that relatively long-serving
    employees whose starting salary was low do not appear to be
    progressing through to higher salaries is worth looking at. Does this
    mean the company is not developing these staff? The correlation is
    moderate at 0.59 and statistically highly significant.

3. To try to answer that question, the data is controlled for job level. Consider the sub-tables to the right. The middle table looks at the relationship between salary levels of those staff in lower levels of the organisation, while that to the right compares the data for staff that joined at a higher level. The pattern appears quite clear. If staff started near the bottom of the jobs structure on lower salaries, they were more likely to stay there. Those whose jobs paid more – perhaps because they required particular skills were twice as likely to progress into the higher salary range than remain in the current lower band. Again this is statistically significant with a correlation of 0.49. The problem comes with the right hand table. Ignore the significance issue for a moment. This table indicates that those who joined the organisation as supervisors and managers five years earlier have been much more successful in progressing through the salary/career scales. It is interesting to note that, while this relationship was statistically significant during when calculating the correlations and multiple regression earlier, the convenient act of collapsing data into dichotomous variables bears a price. Note, too, that half the cells have a frequency less than 5, making it suspect anyway. You will only be able to support the explanation by using the correlation matrix generated earlier.

You may be able to get over the problem of significance by collapsing the data into three categories (low, medium and high) or by selecting different cut-off values (e.g. the mean rather than median). However, this does demonstrate a major difficulty with collapsing data, as discussed in chapter 7.

Tutorial: helping you learn

Progress questions
1. Why do you construct a correlation matrix of all the non-nominal variables in your study?

2. What is the purpose of a partial correlation, and how do you interpret the results of this procedure?

3. What is the purpose of multiple regression, and how do you interpret the output from the procedure?

4. When you use the STEPWISE method in multiple regression, why is it that one or more of the variables you instructed the software to use may not appear in the analysis? Why is the use of bivariate tables (cross-tabulations) to be recommended in demonstrating the effect of a moderating variable even though it is probably less precise and may not show the true strength of association?

Discussion points

Discuss the relative merits of the approach to analysing non-nominal data described in this chapter, and also why an over-enthusiastic use of multiple regression should be avoided. To what extent can the social sciences claim to be able to provide predictive data?

Assignment

Access the web site that accompanies this book. In the section for this chapter you will find a data set and tasks to carry out with the data. Please be warned: the tasks are challenging and you should work with one or two other people. This is usually the approach taken in research where a small team, each person with a particular expertise or ability, can solve problems more effectively than an individual.

Study tip

As this book is an introductory text on data analysis for the social sciences, the techniques in this chapter are fairly advanced for the novice researcher without a statistics background. If you find the concepts surrounding these techniques difficult, don't be surprised or alarmed. Re-read chapters 9 and 10, where the underlying principles have been described, and then come back to this chapter.

Web Sites for Social Science Students

One-minute Overview – The internet, or world wide web, is an amazingly useful resource, giving the student nearly free and almost immediate information on any topic. Ignore this vast and valuable store of materials at your peril! The following list of web sites may be helpful for you. Please note that neither the author nor the publisher is responsible for content or opinions expressed on the sites listed, which are simply intended to offer starting points for students. Also, remember that the internet is a fast-evolving environment, and links may come and go. If you have some favourite sites you would like to see mentioned in future editions of this book, please write to Ian Hosker c/o Studymates (address on back cover), or email him at the address shown below. You will find a free selection of useful and readymade student links at the Studymates web site. Happy surfing!

Studymates web site: http://www.studymates.co.uk
Ian Hosker email: ian.hosker@studymates.co.uk

Social statistics

Here are some recommended web sites with information on social statistics:

OECD Statistics
http://www.oecd.org
This is a page of the Organisation for Economic Co-operation and Development. It deals with such topics as economic statistics, agriculture, energy, development, co-operation, public management, education and labour.

Office for National Statistics
http://www.statistics.gov.uk
This is the principal home page for government statistical information.

Royal Statistical Society
http://www.rss.org.uk/
The RSS is the professional body for statisticians practising in industry, commerce, government, education, or research.

UK Government
http://www.direct.gov.uk
This is the home page of the UK government. All government departments can be accessed from this page.

Index